THE INCREDIBLE HULK™

AN ORIGIN STORY

Based on the Marvel comic book series The Hulk

Adapted by Rich Thomas

Interior Illustrated by Val Semeiks *and* Hi-Fi Design

MARVEL
New York

visit us at www.abdopublishing.com

Reinforced library bound edition published in 2013 by Spotlight, a division of the ABDO Group, PO Box 398166, Minneapolis, MN 55439. Spotlight produces high-quality reinforced library bound editions for schools and libraries. Published by agreement with Marvel Press, an imprint of Disney Book Group, LLC.

Printed in the United States of America, North Mankato, Minnesota.
042012
052013
This book contains at least 10% recycled materials.

For Peter's little super heroes,
Max and Lucy
—RT

TM & © 2012 Marvel & Subs.

Library of Congress Cataloging-in-Publication Data

This book was previously cataloged with the following information:
Thomas, Richard.
The incredible hulk origin storybook / [edited by] Michael Siglain, Tomas Palacios.
p. cm.
1. Incredible Hulk (Fictitious character)—Juvenile fiction. 2. Superheroes—Juvenile fiction.
3. Scientists—Juvenile fiction. 4. Good and evil—Juvenile fiction. I. Title.
PZ7.T36933 2012
[E]-dc223

2010938844

ISBN 978-1-61479-009-9 (reinforced library edition)

All Spotlight books are reinforced library binding
and manufactured in the United States of America.

marvelkids.co

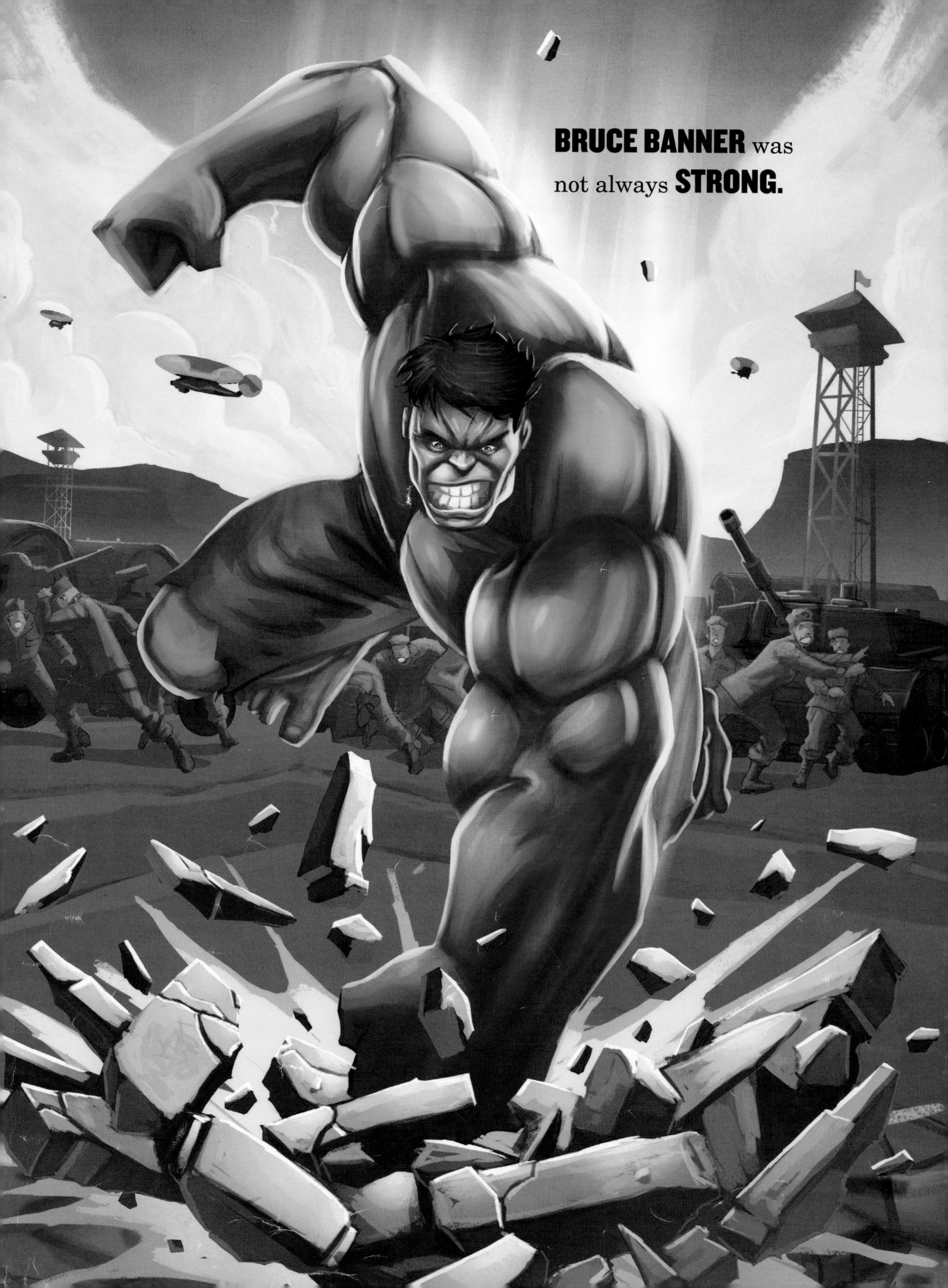

BRUCE BANNER was not always **STRONG.**

He was not always **POWERFUL.**

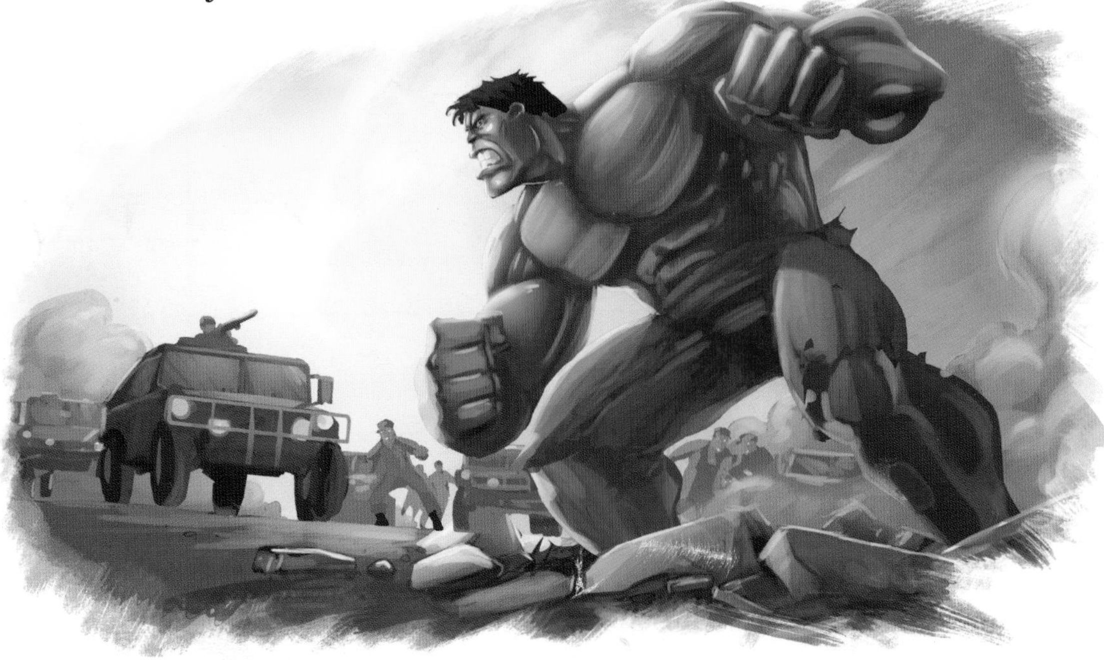

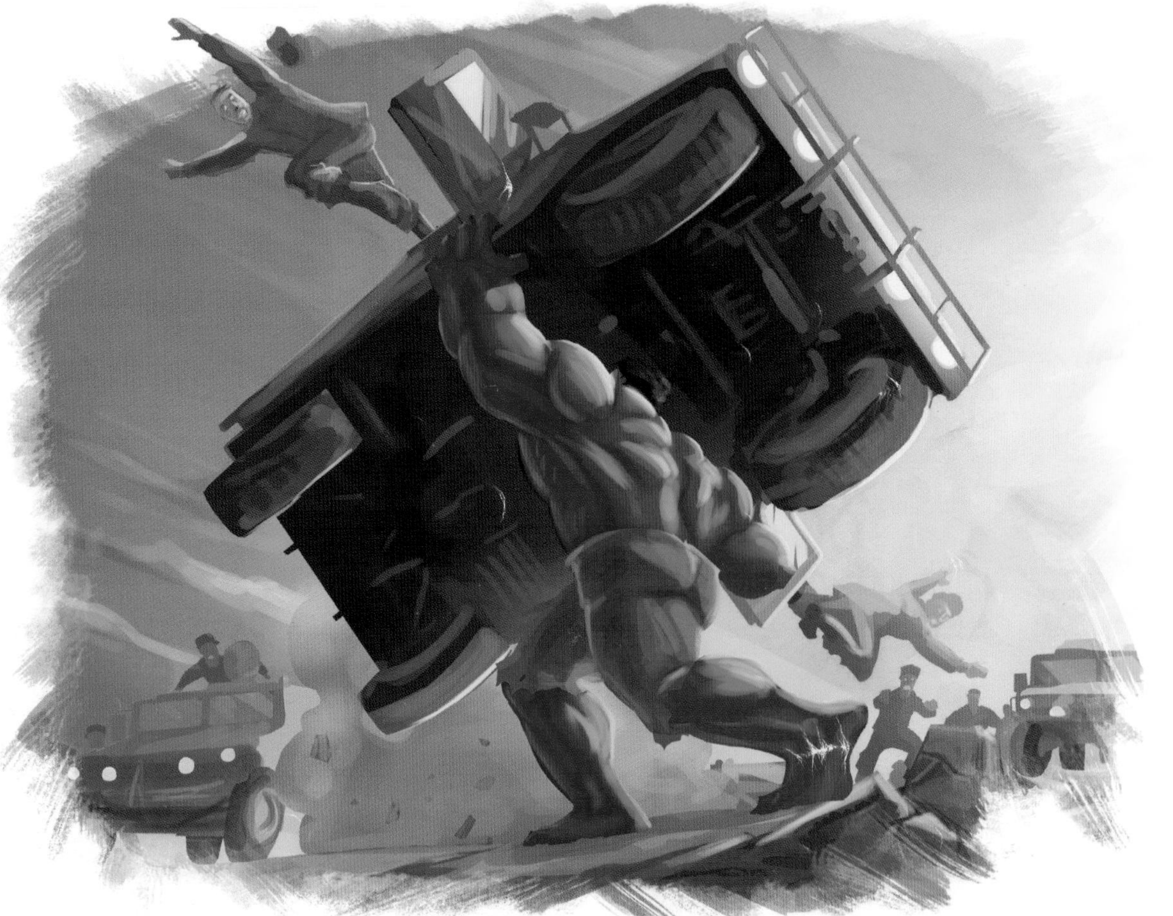

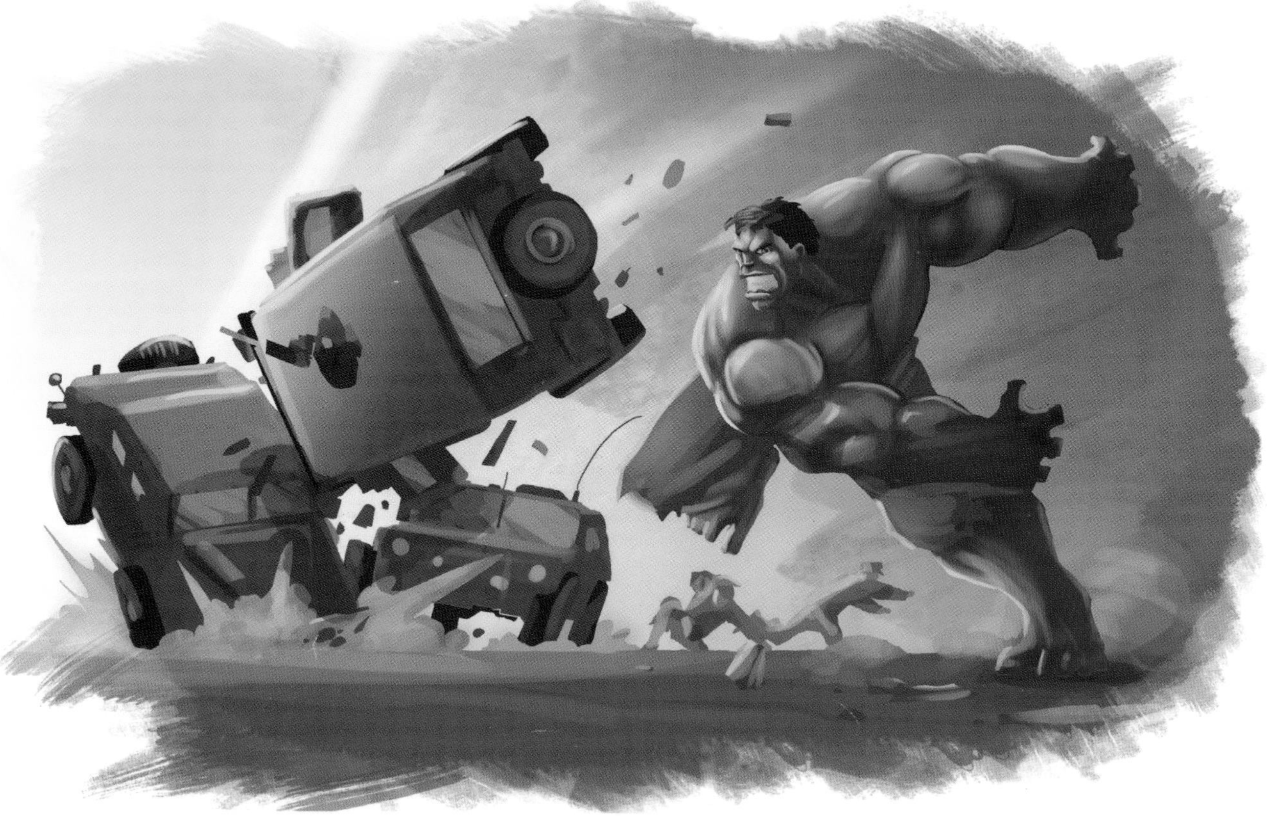

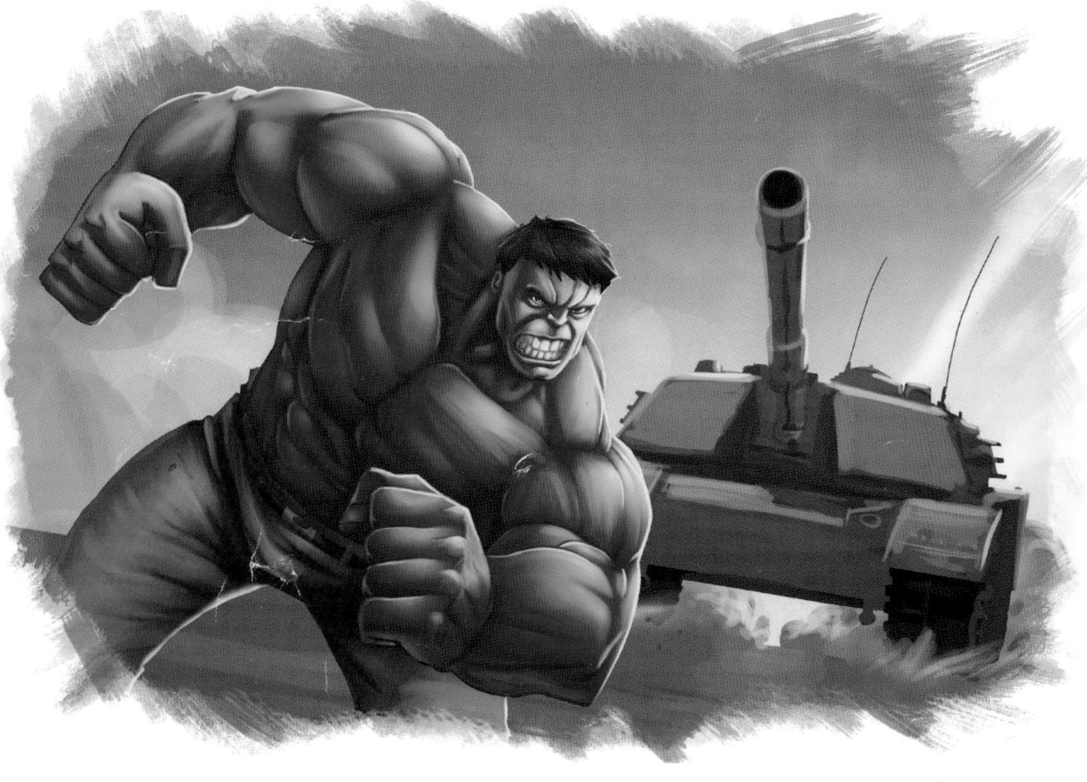

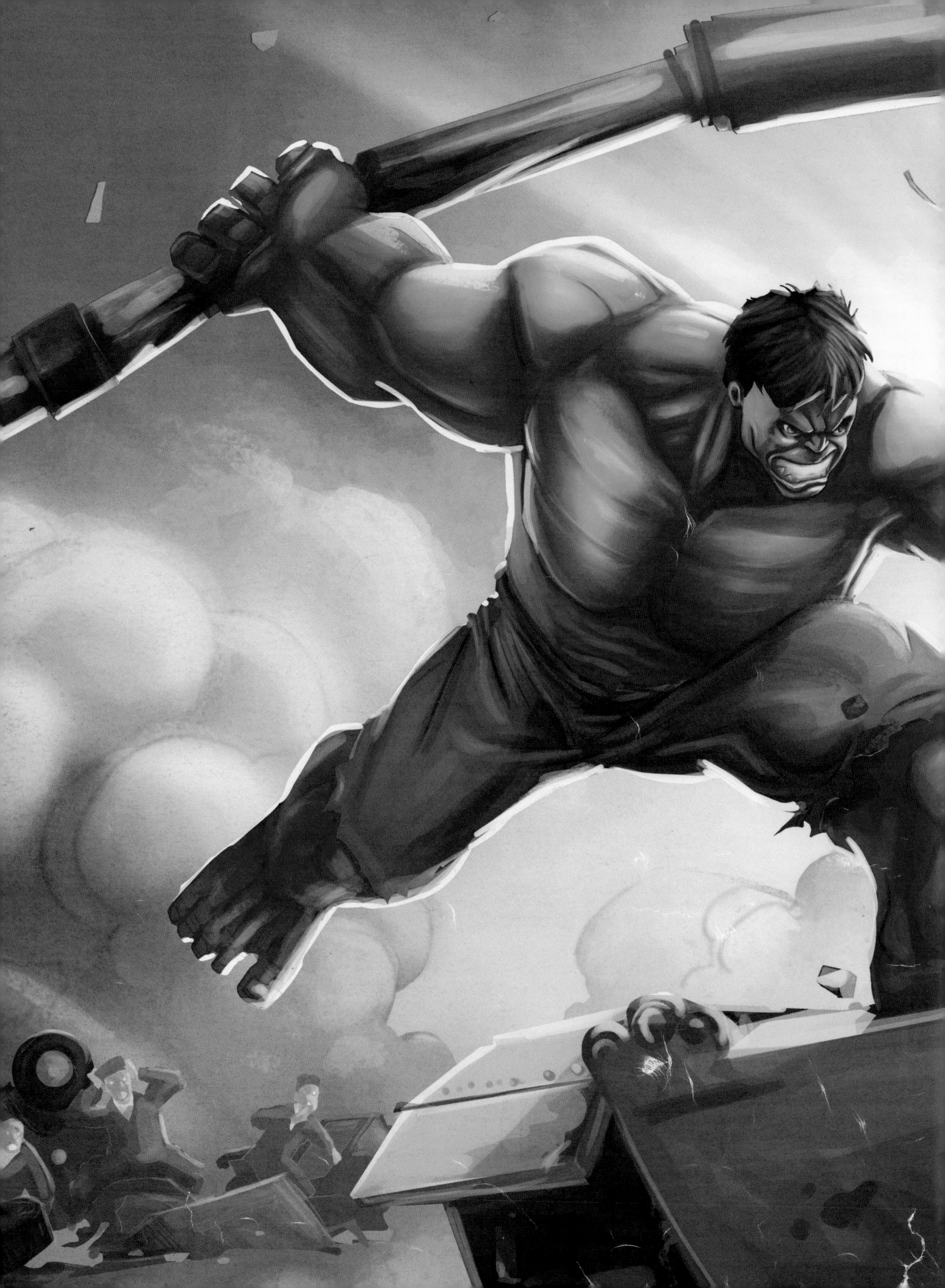

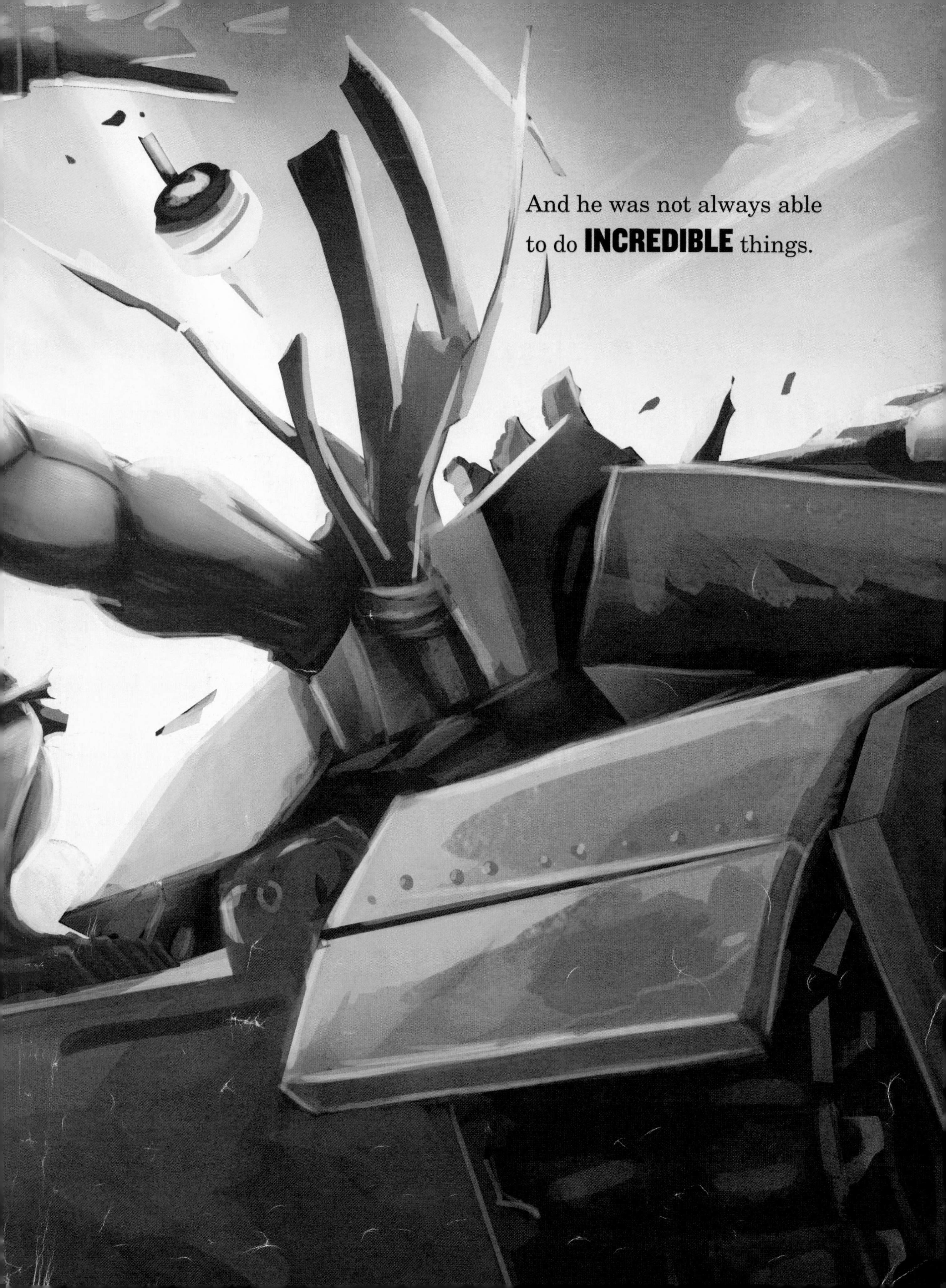

And he was not always able to do **INCREDIBLE** things.

But most of all, Bruce was not always feared.

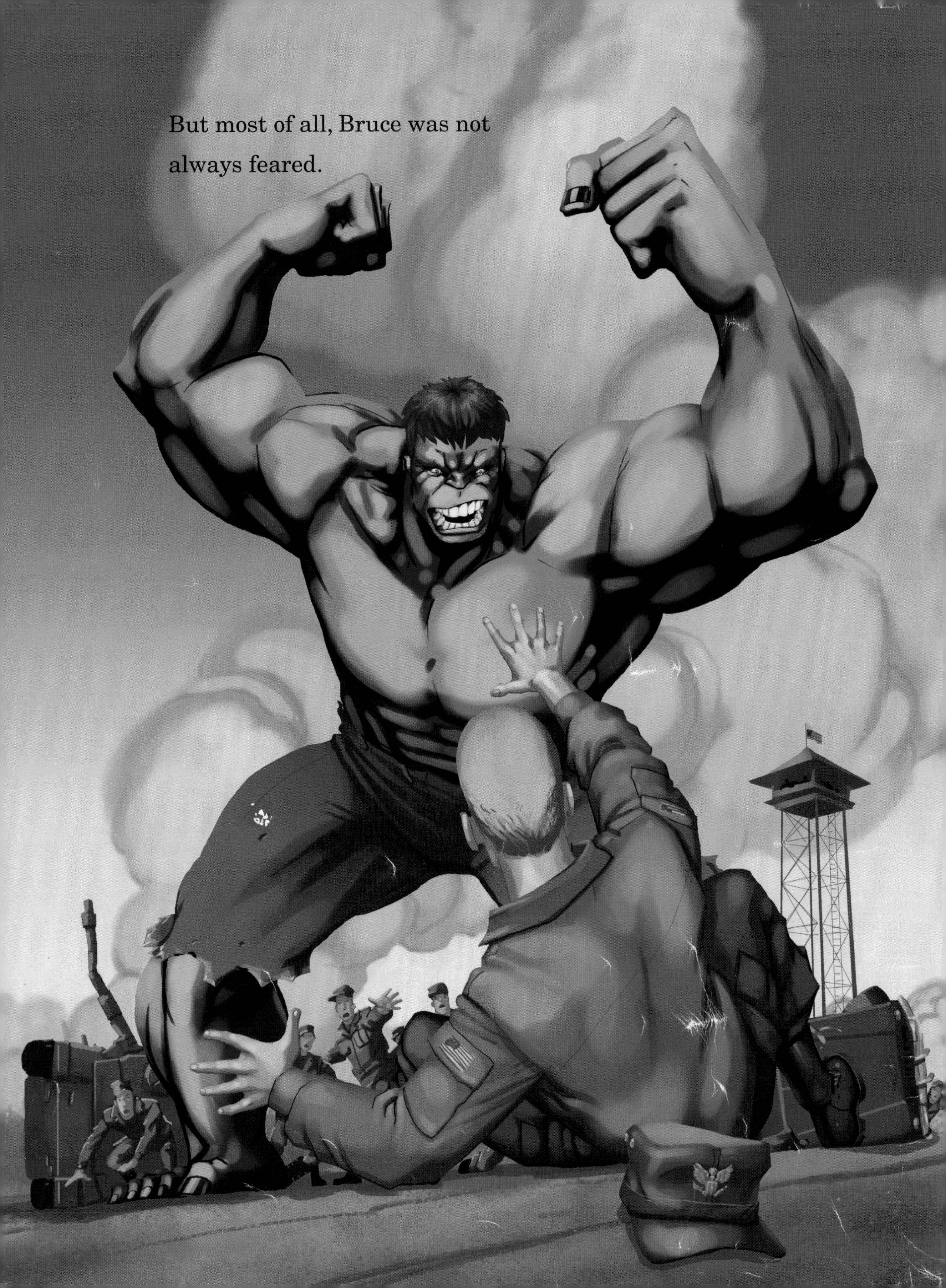

In fact, when he was young,

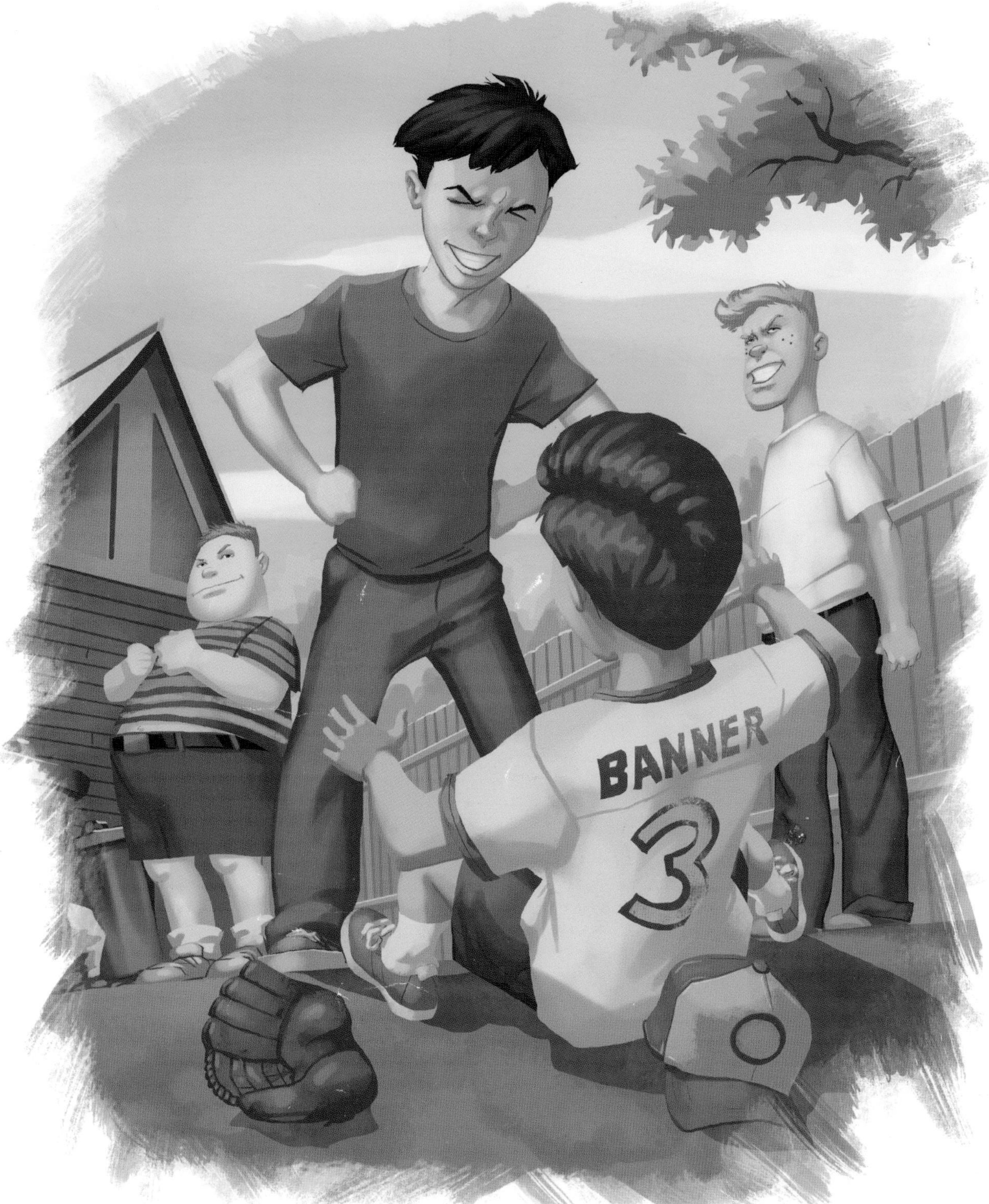
BANNER
3

Bruce was mostly **AFRAID.**

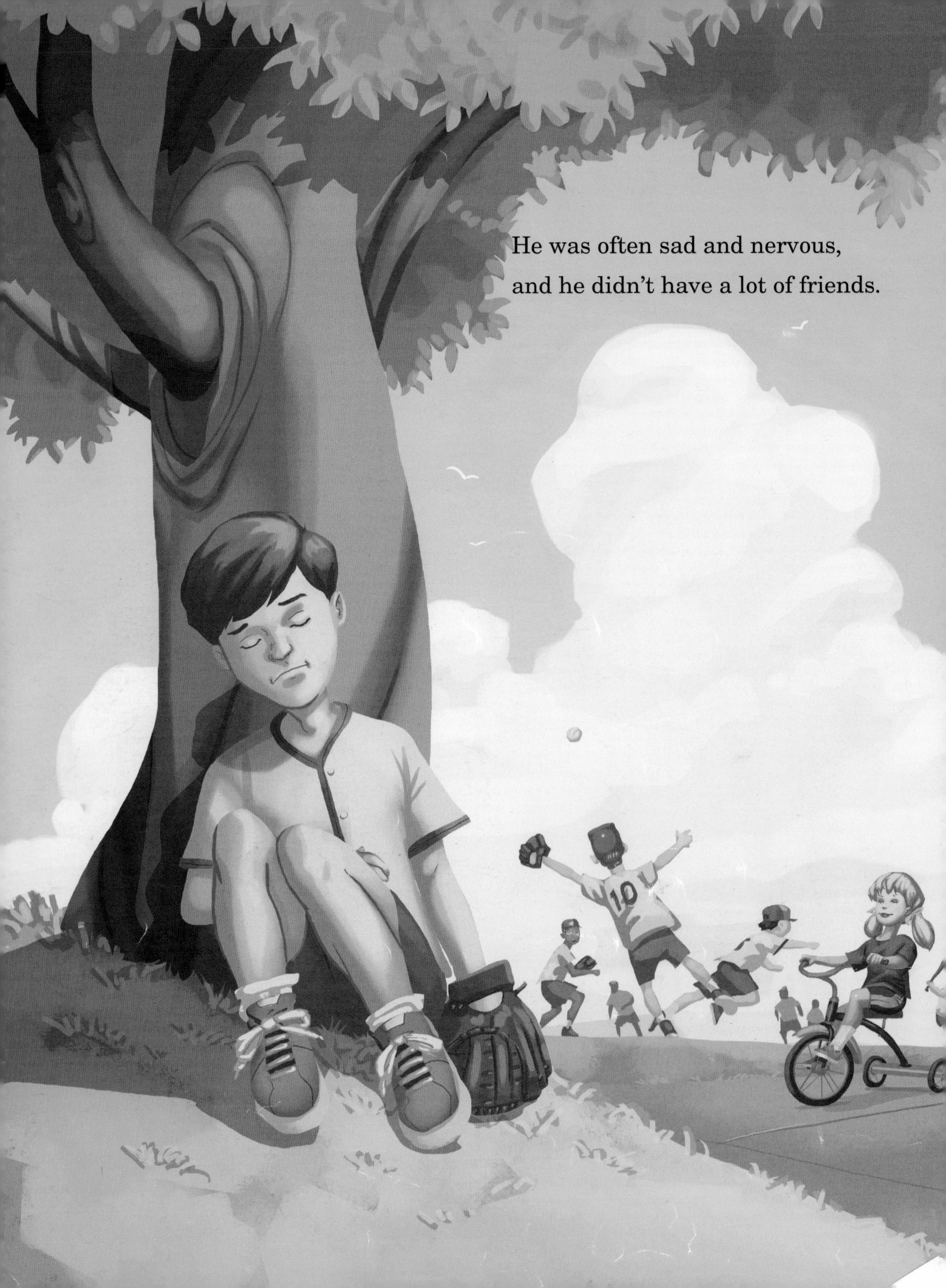
10

He was often sad and nervous,
and he didn't have a lot of friends.

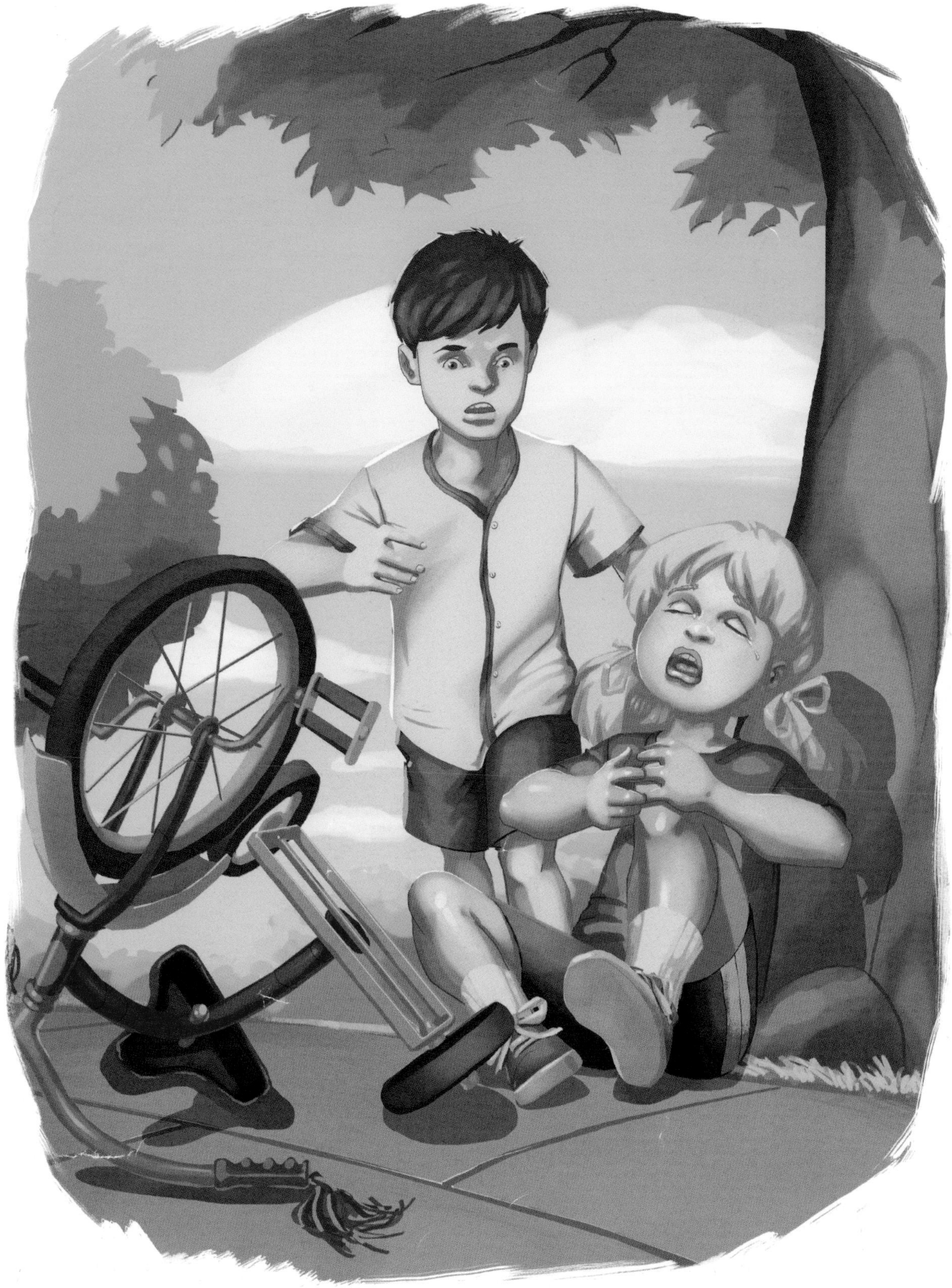

But he was always ready to **HELP** someone in need.

Bruce kept all his feelings
buried deep inside him.

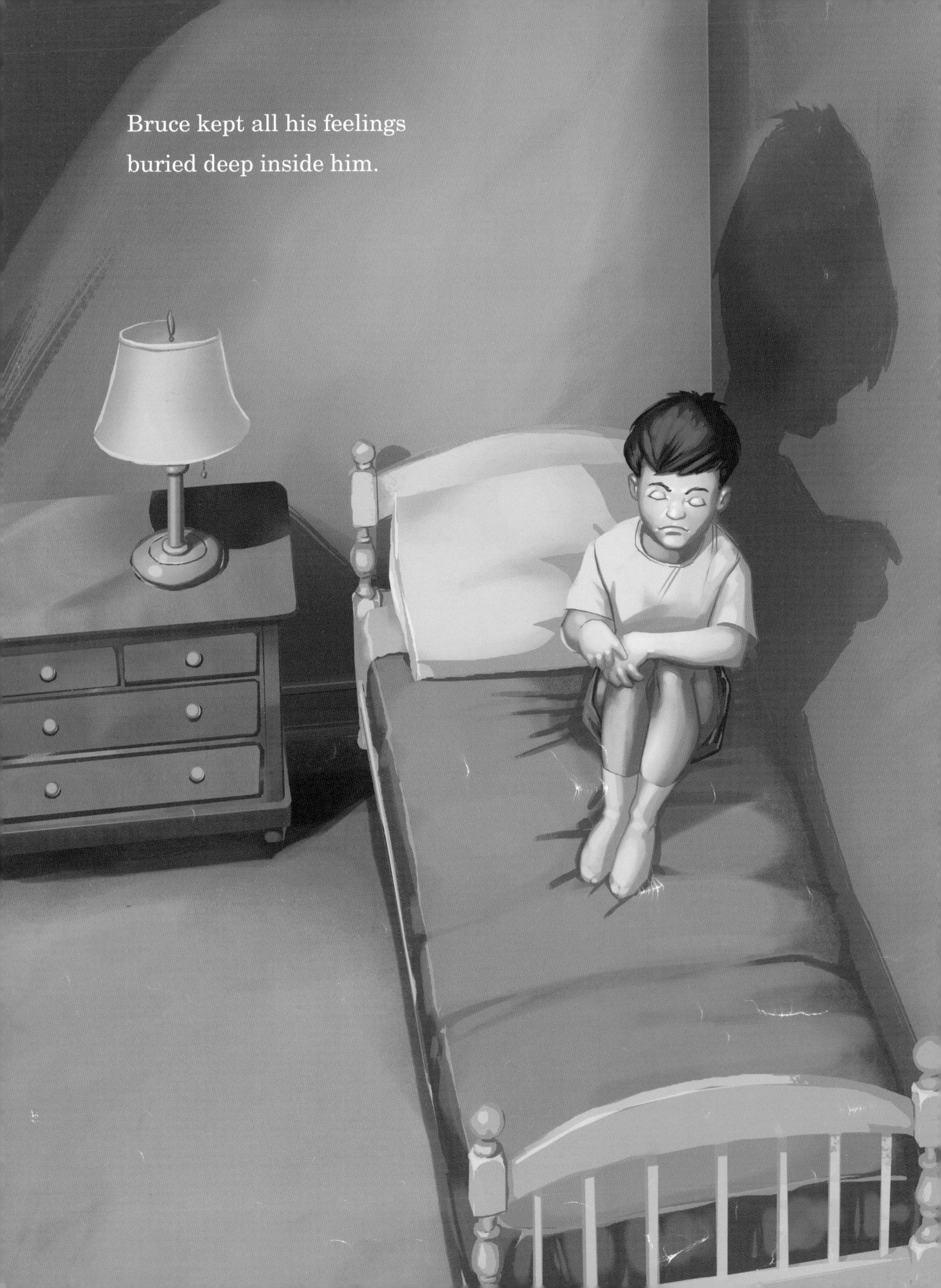

Reading books about **SCIENCE** always took his mind off things.

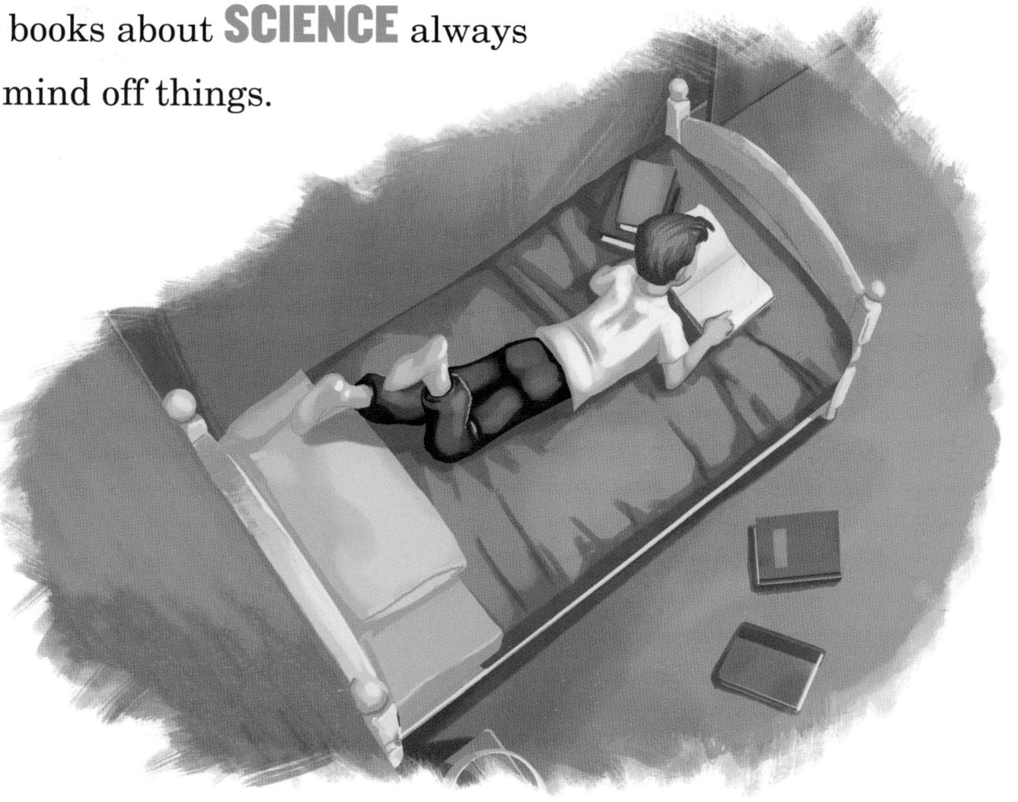

And so, Bruce spent an awful lot of time with those books.

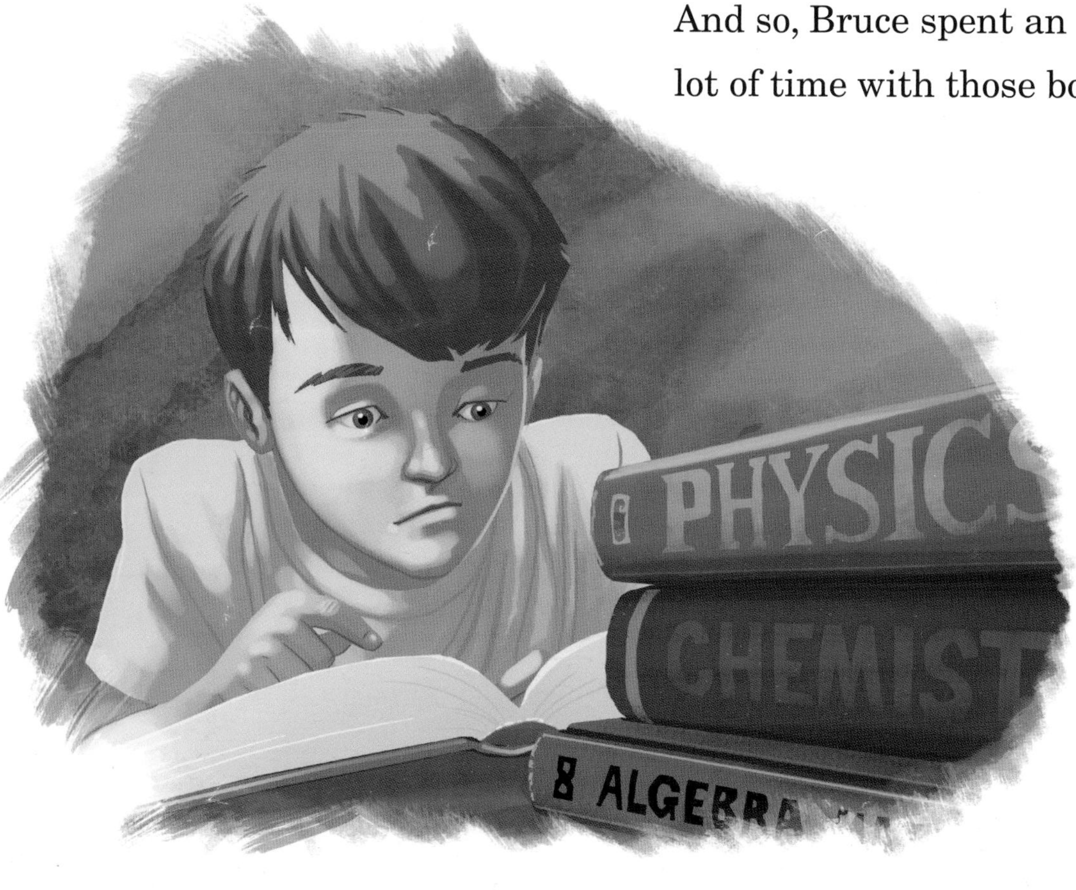
PHYSICS
CHEMIST
8 ALGEBRA

As Bruce grew older . . .

. . . he continued to read, study, and learn . . .

. . . but he never learned how to talk about his **FEELINGS.**

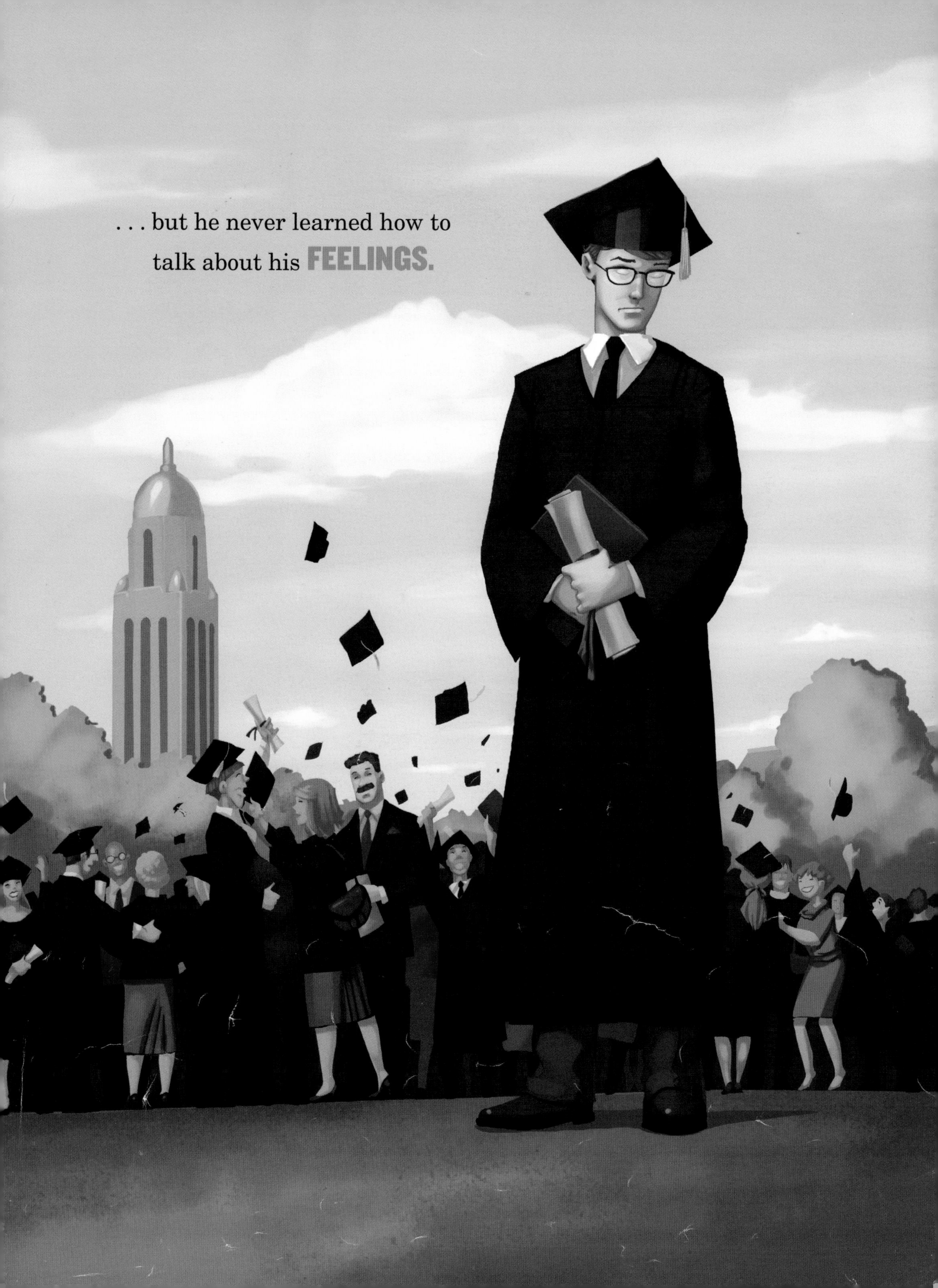

Bruce became a doctor of science who worked for the army.
He worked very hard both day and night.

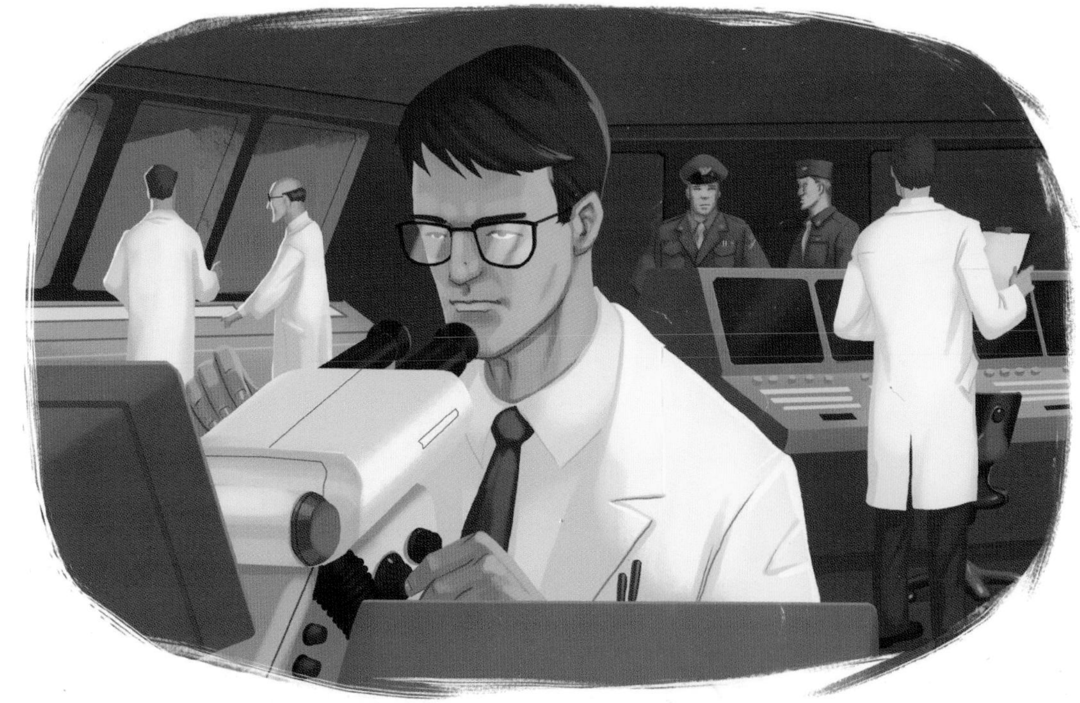

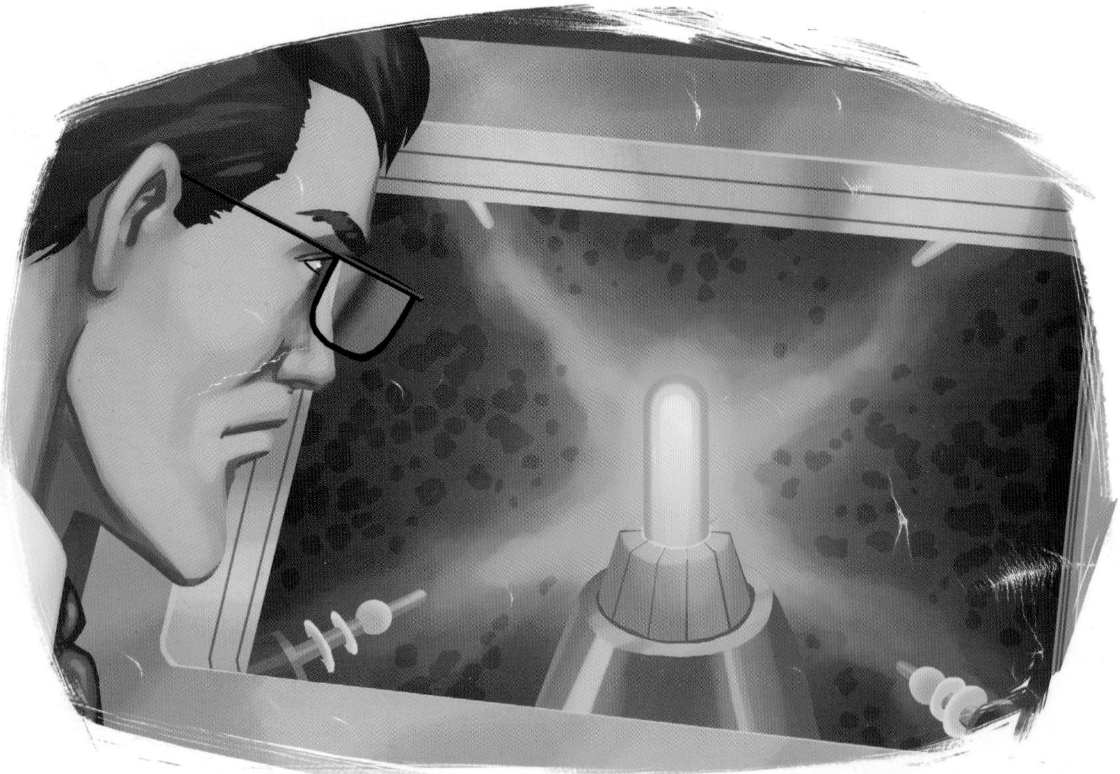

He was studying a type of energy called **GAMMA RADIATION.**

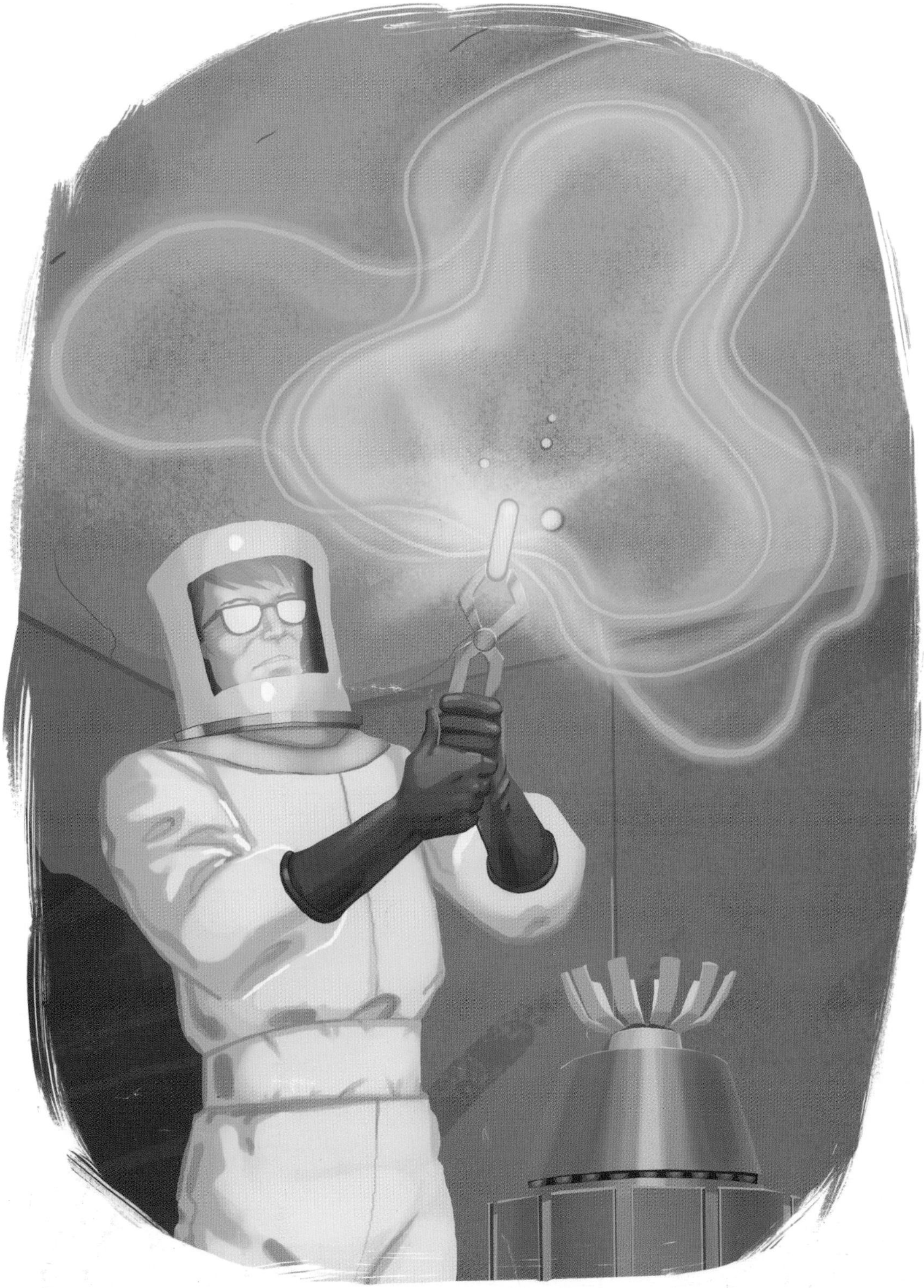

It was very dangerous, so he needed to be careful when he was near it. He wanted to find a way to use its power for **GOOD.**

Bruce decided the best way to test the gamma rays' power was to cause a massive explosion.

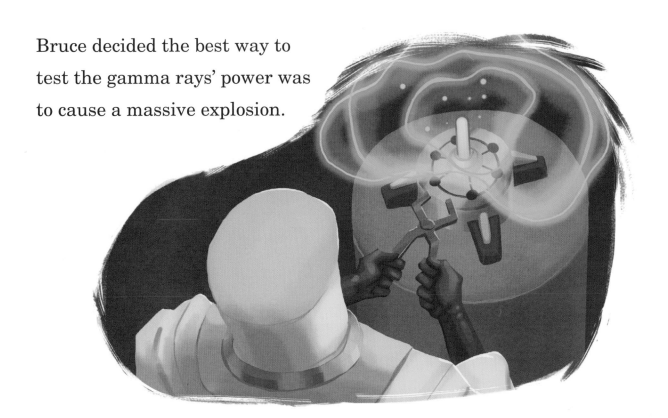

He would then measure the dangerous gamma radiation with special equipment.

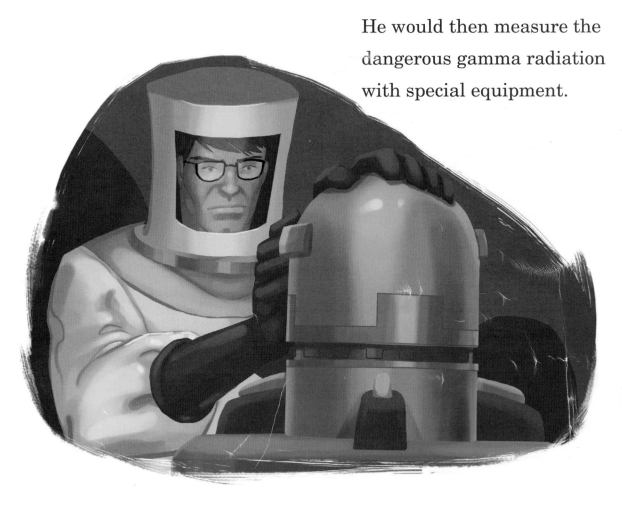

GENERAL "THUNDERBOLT" ROSS was in charge of the army lab where Bruce worked. He was angry with Bruce. The general had been waiting far too long to find out how much power the gamma rays held.

He needed to know. **RIGHT NOW!**

But Bruce needed time to make sure the device was safe. He did not want anyone to get hurt. This made General Ross even angrier, and he yelled at Bruce some more.

Deep inside, Bruce remembered how upset he felt when people yelled at him as a kid.

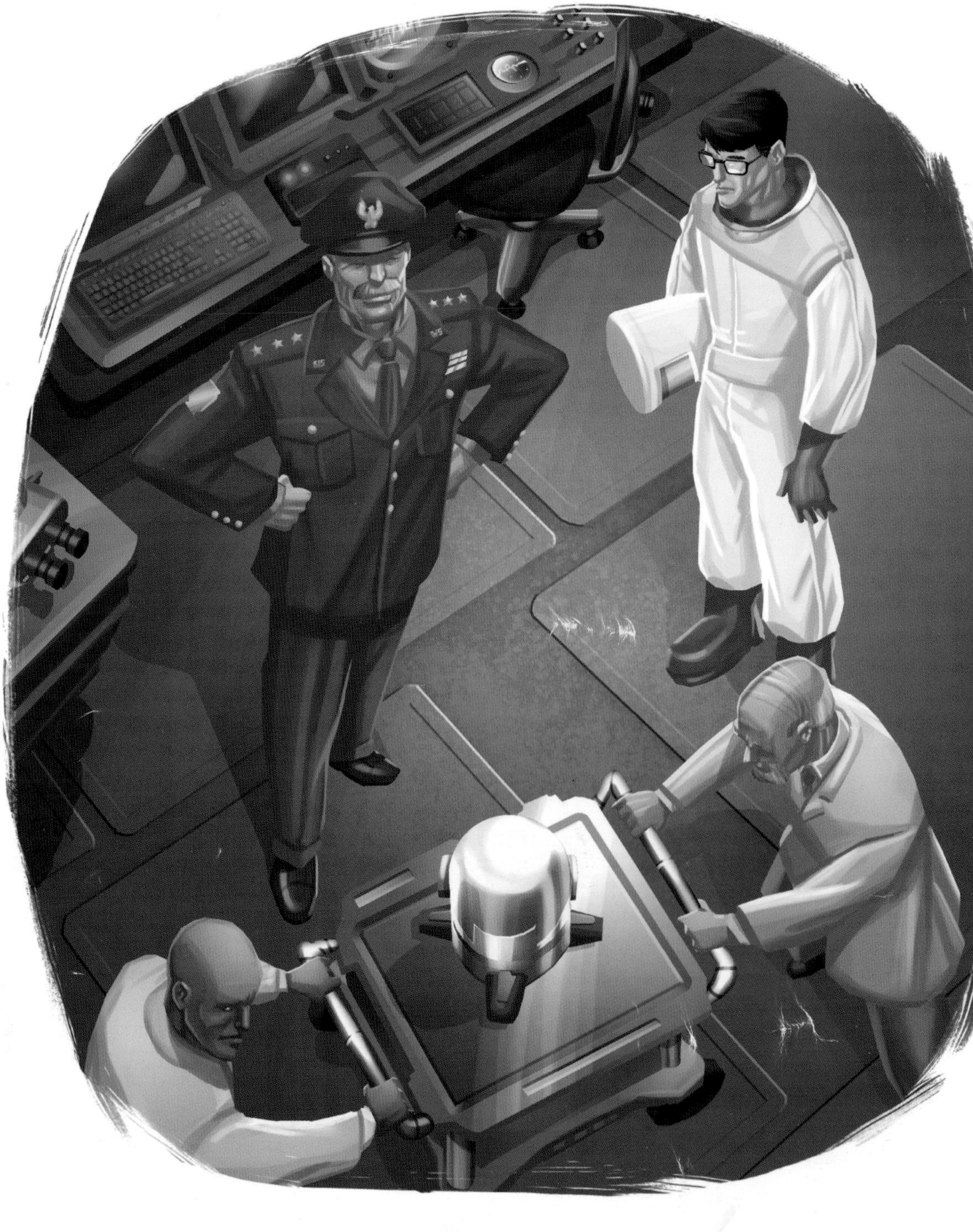

So he listened to the general's orders and sent the device to a safe area in the desert to be tested.

Soon, the countdown began.

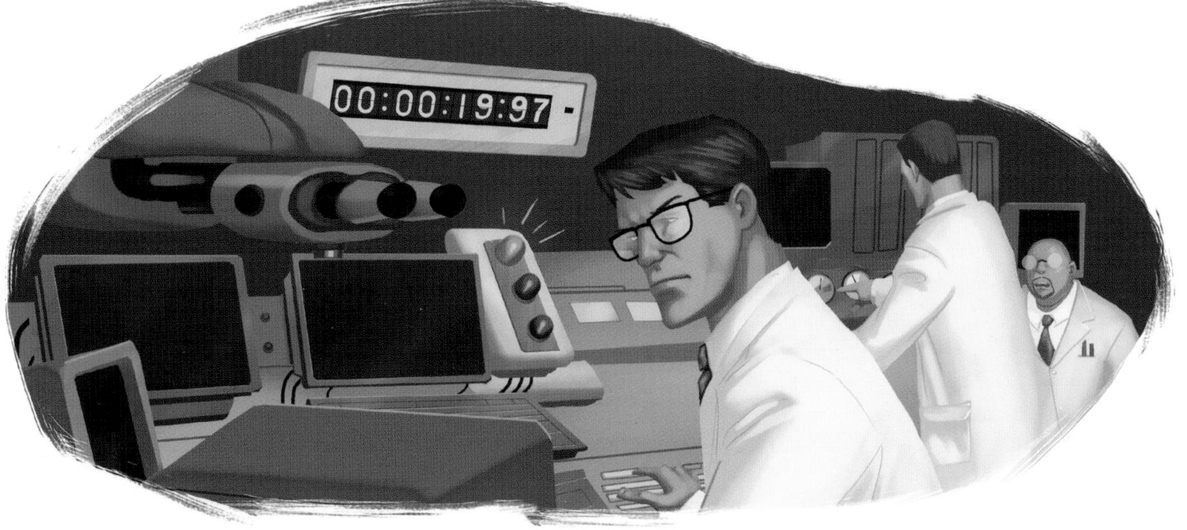
00:00:19:97

But just then, Bruce noticed something on his computer screen.
He looked through his telescope to see what was wrong.

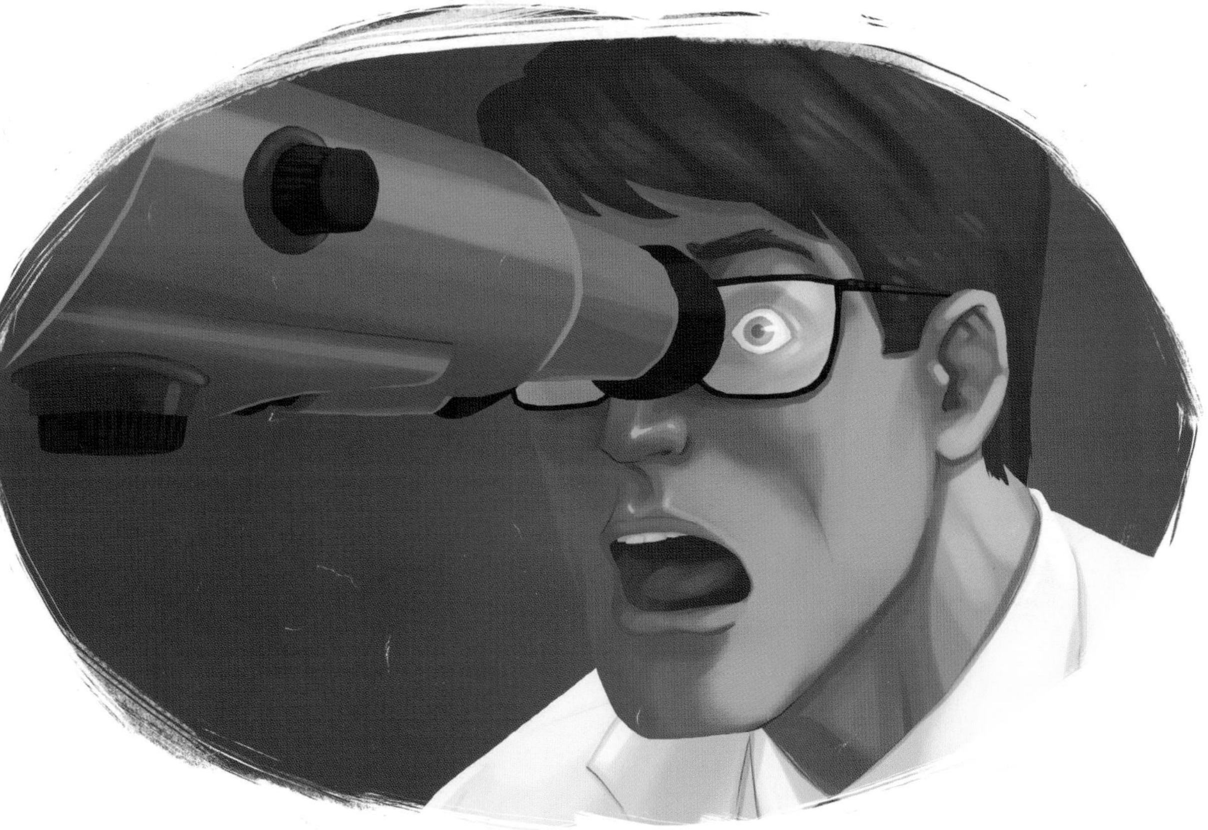

Someone had driven right into the danger zone!

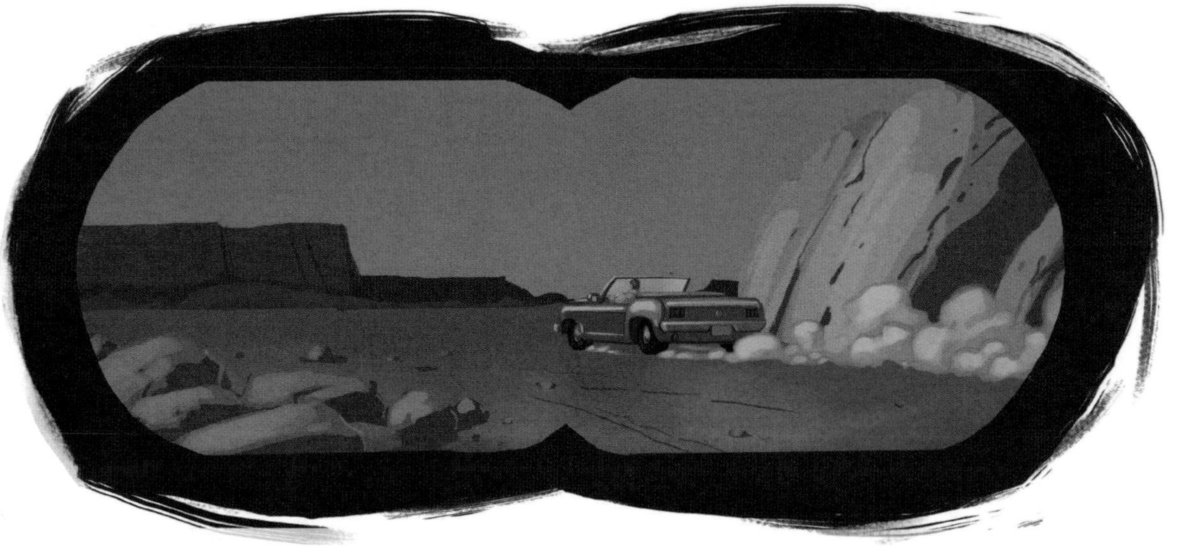

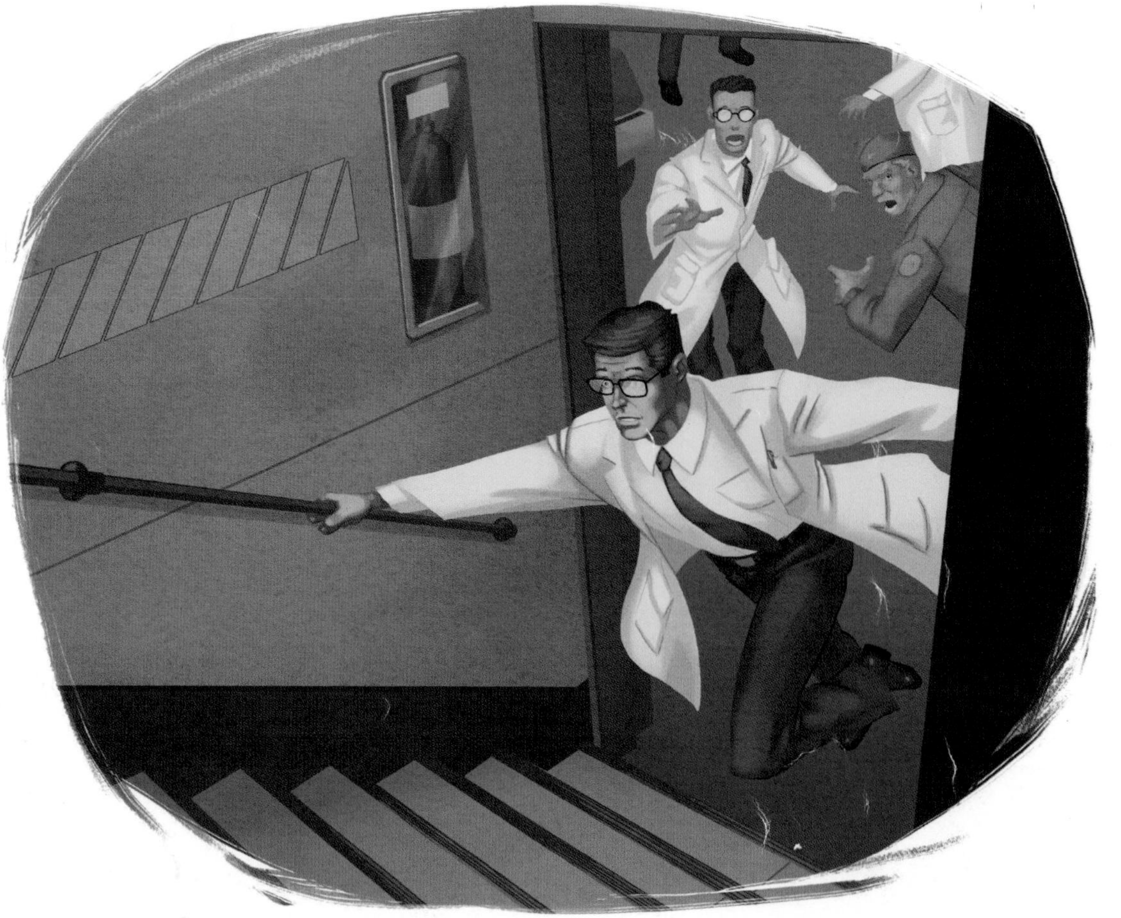

Bruce rushed out of the lab.

He couldn’t let anyone be hurt by his experiment.

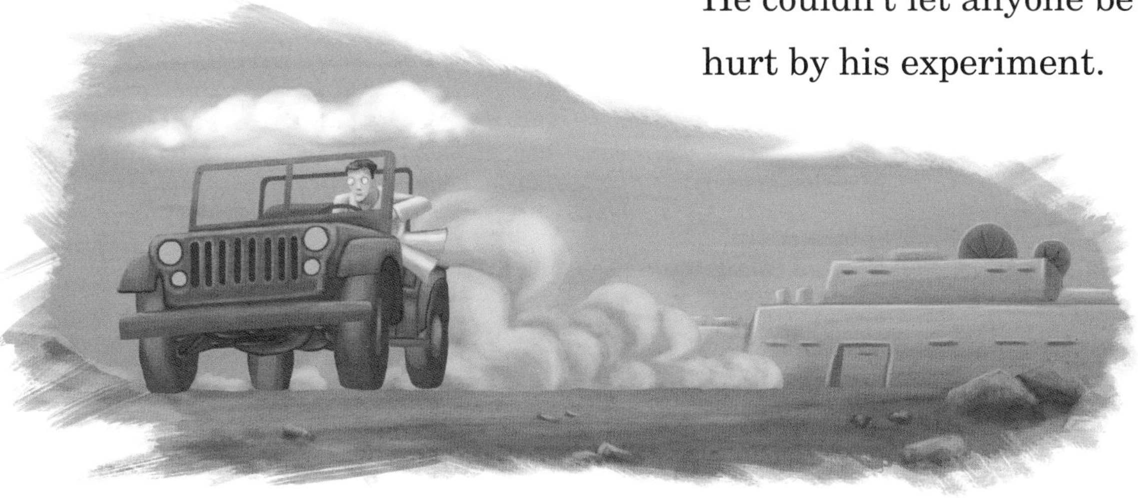

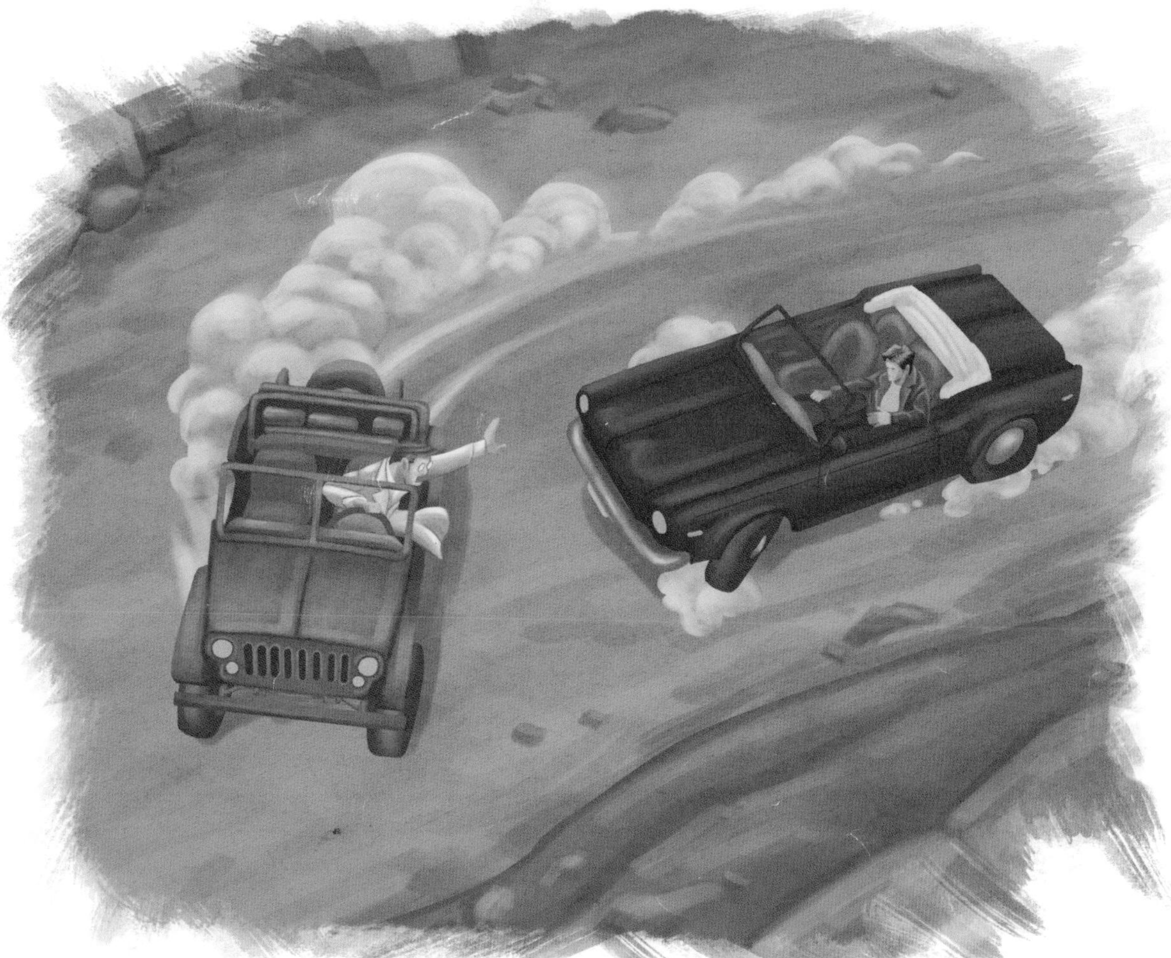

Bruce told the teenager in the car that he needed to leave the site **RIGHT AWAY.**

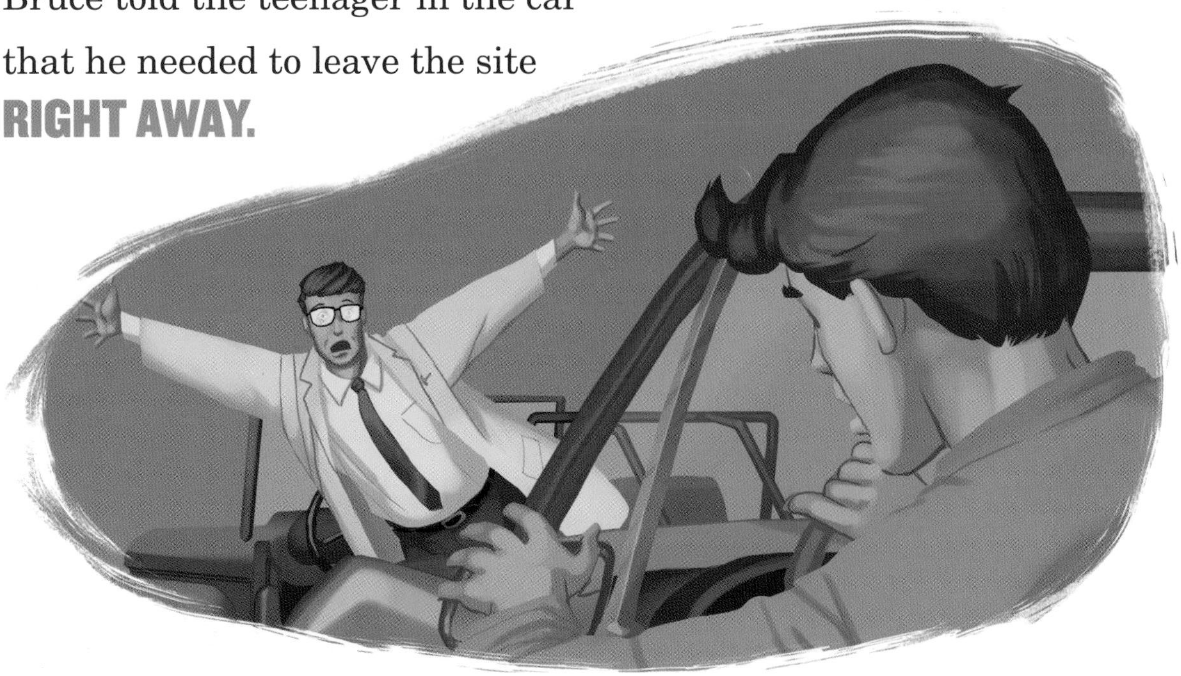

But Bruce quickly realized they did not have time to clear the area!

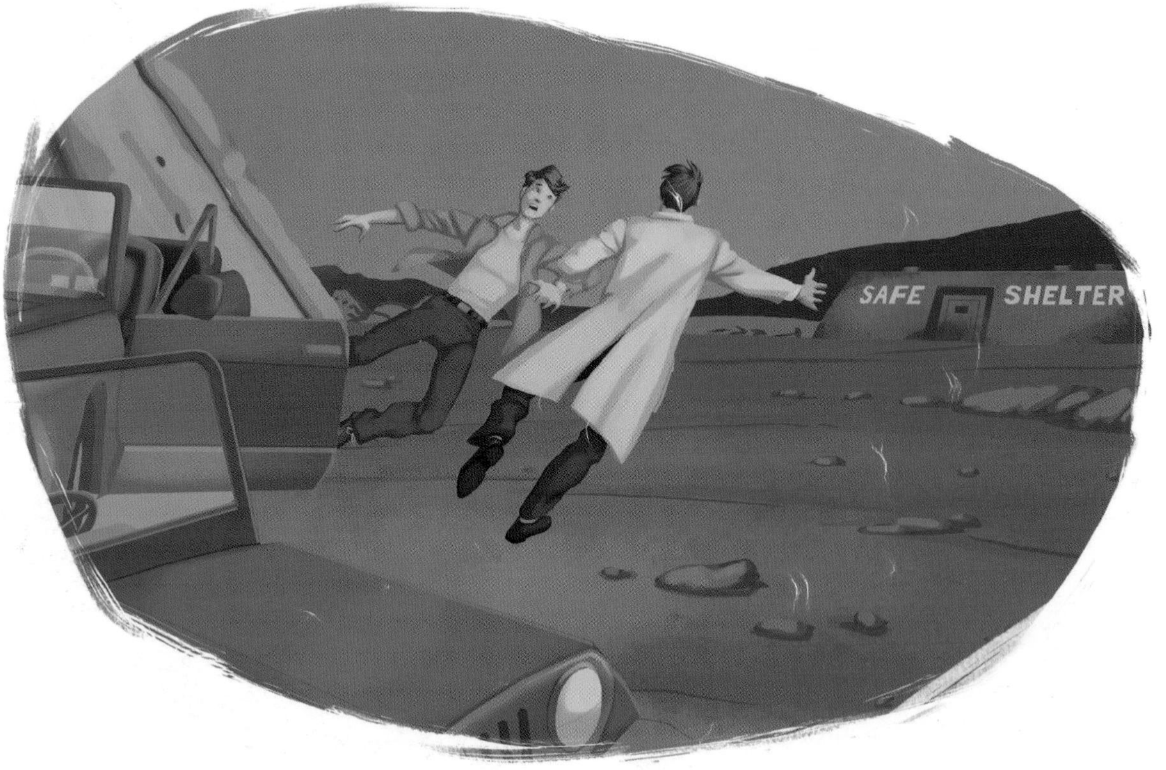
SAFE
SHELTER

He pushed the boy to safety inside a nearby shelter.

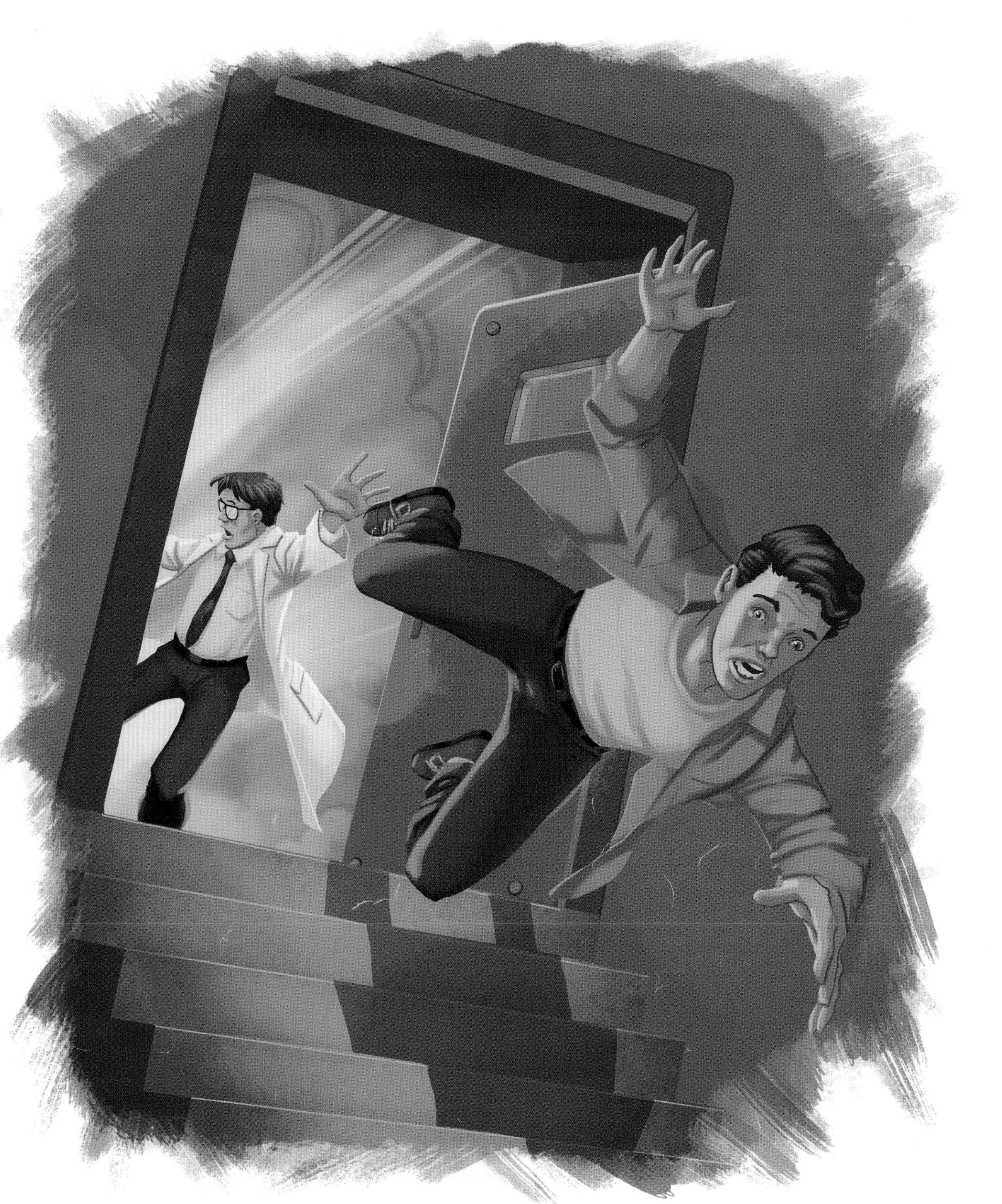

5...4...3...

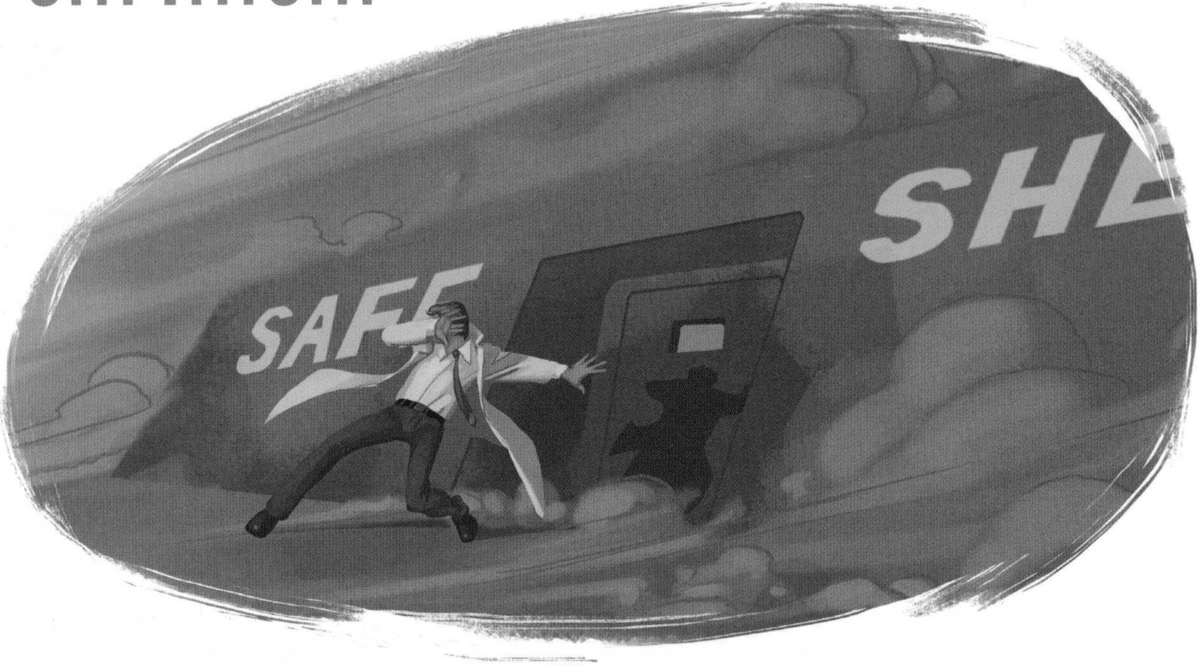
SAFE

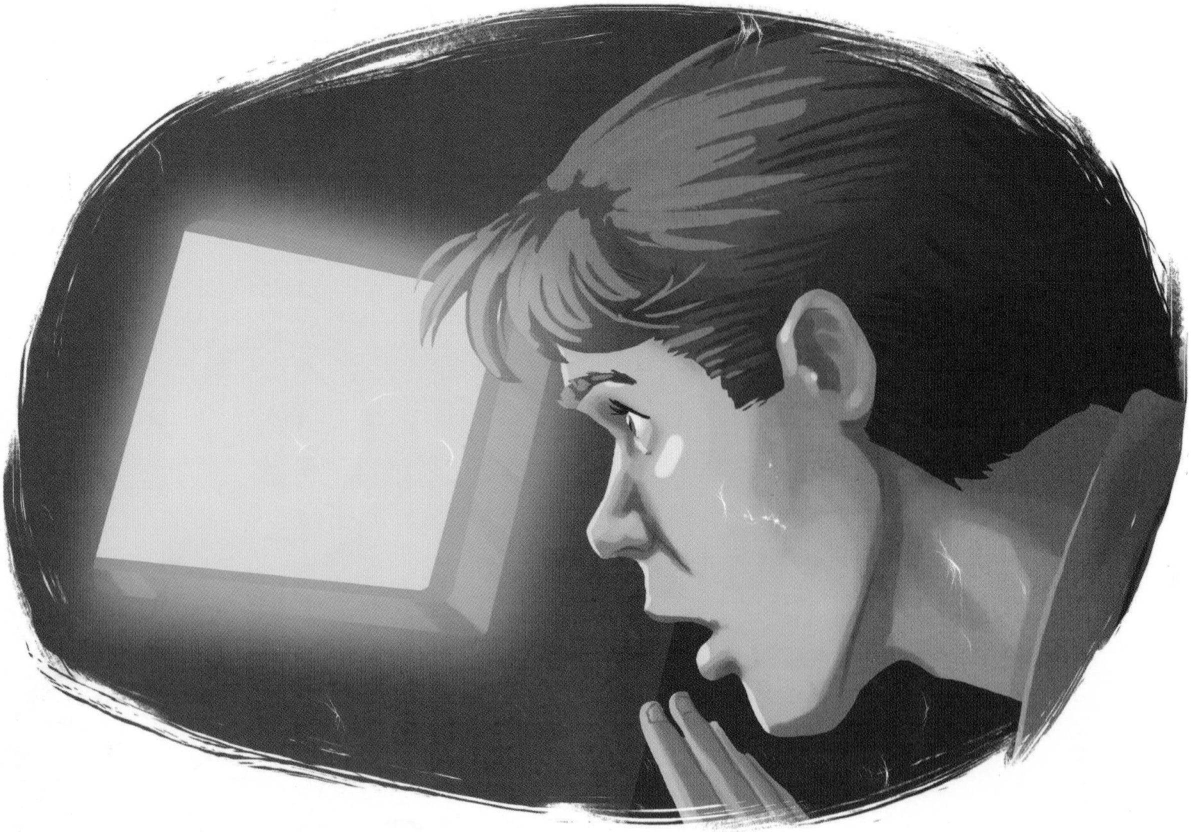

2...1...

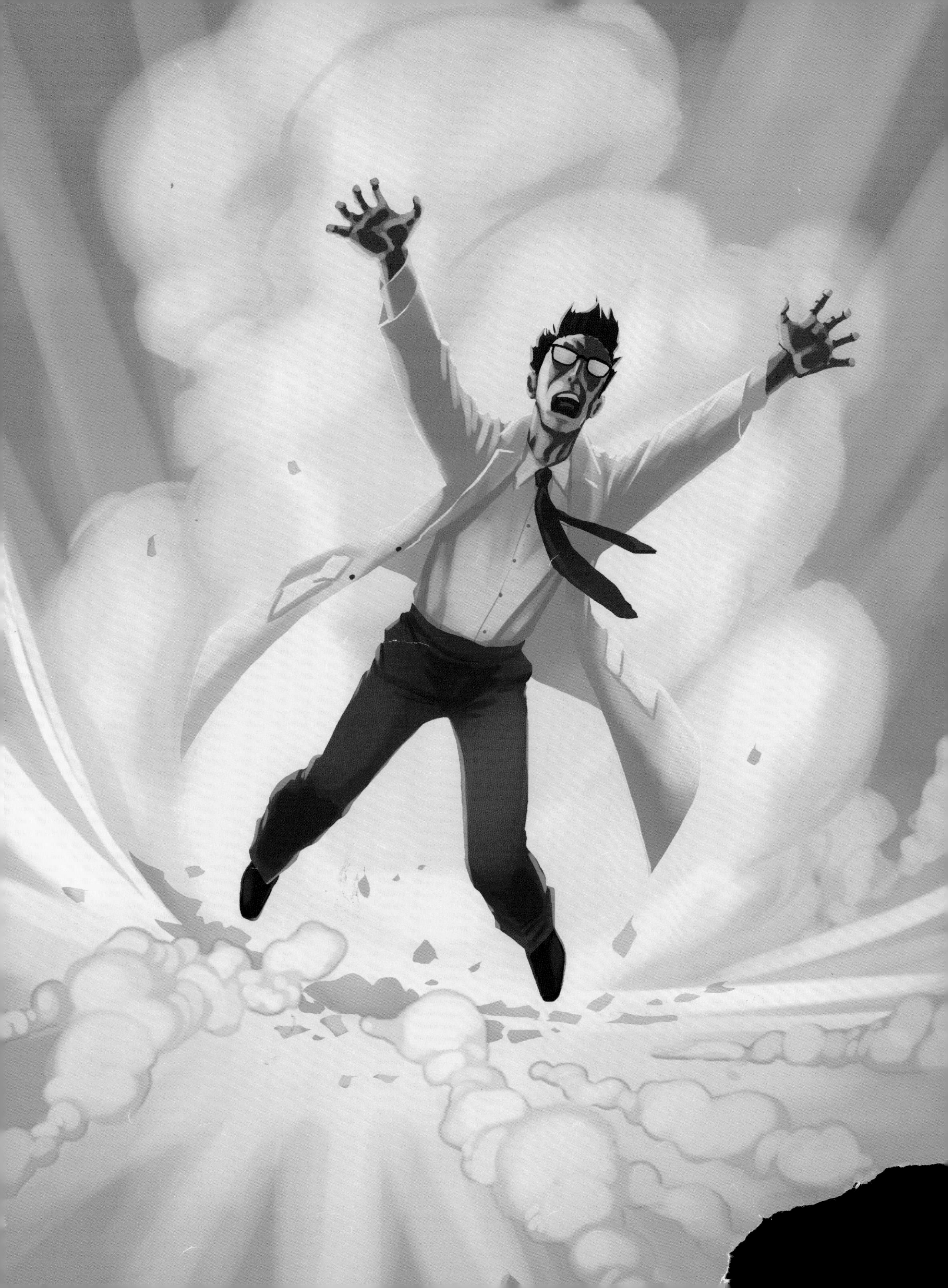

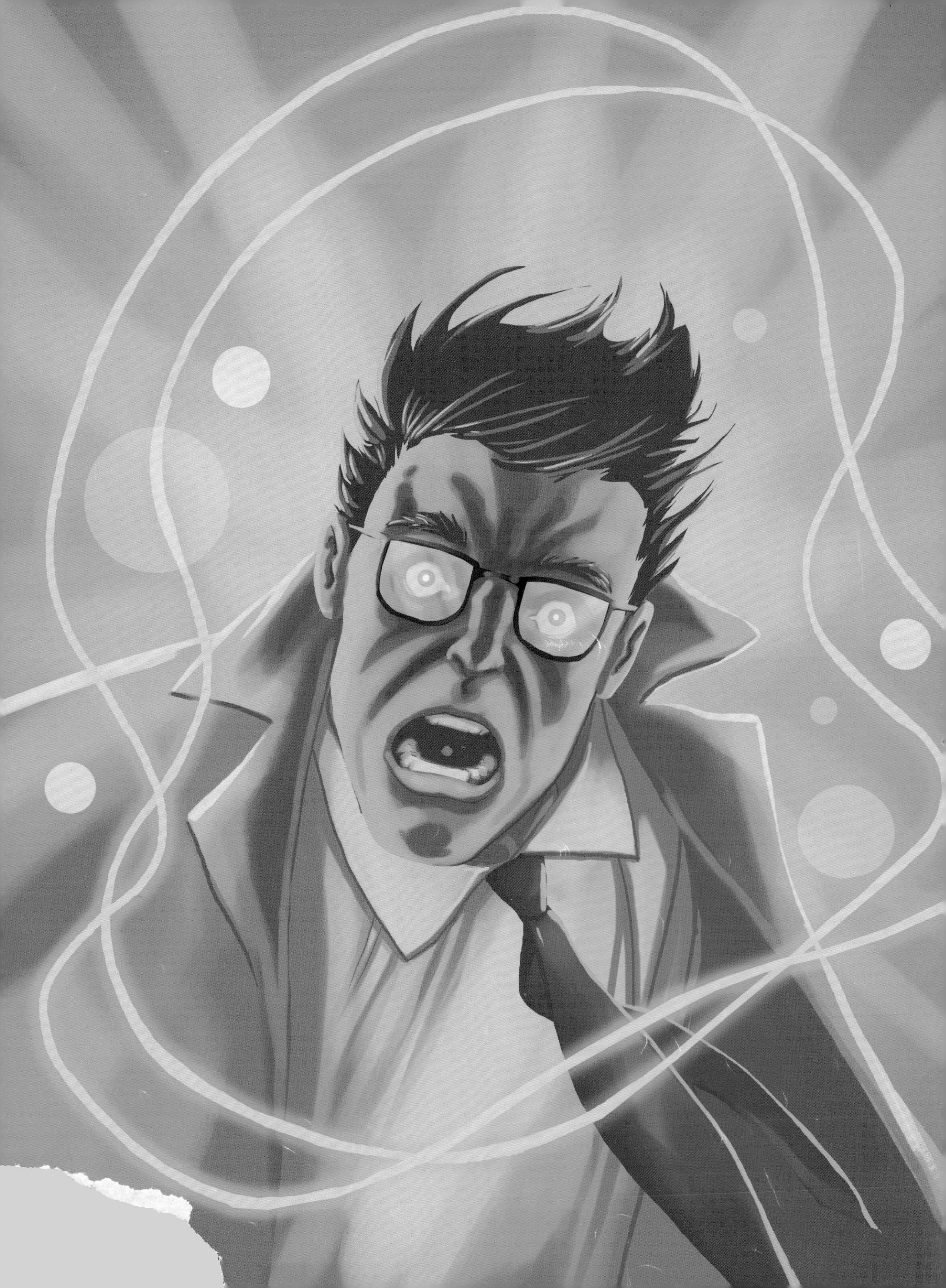

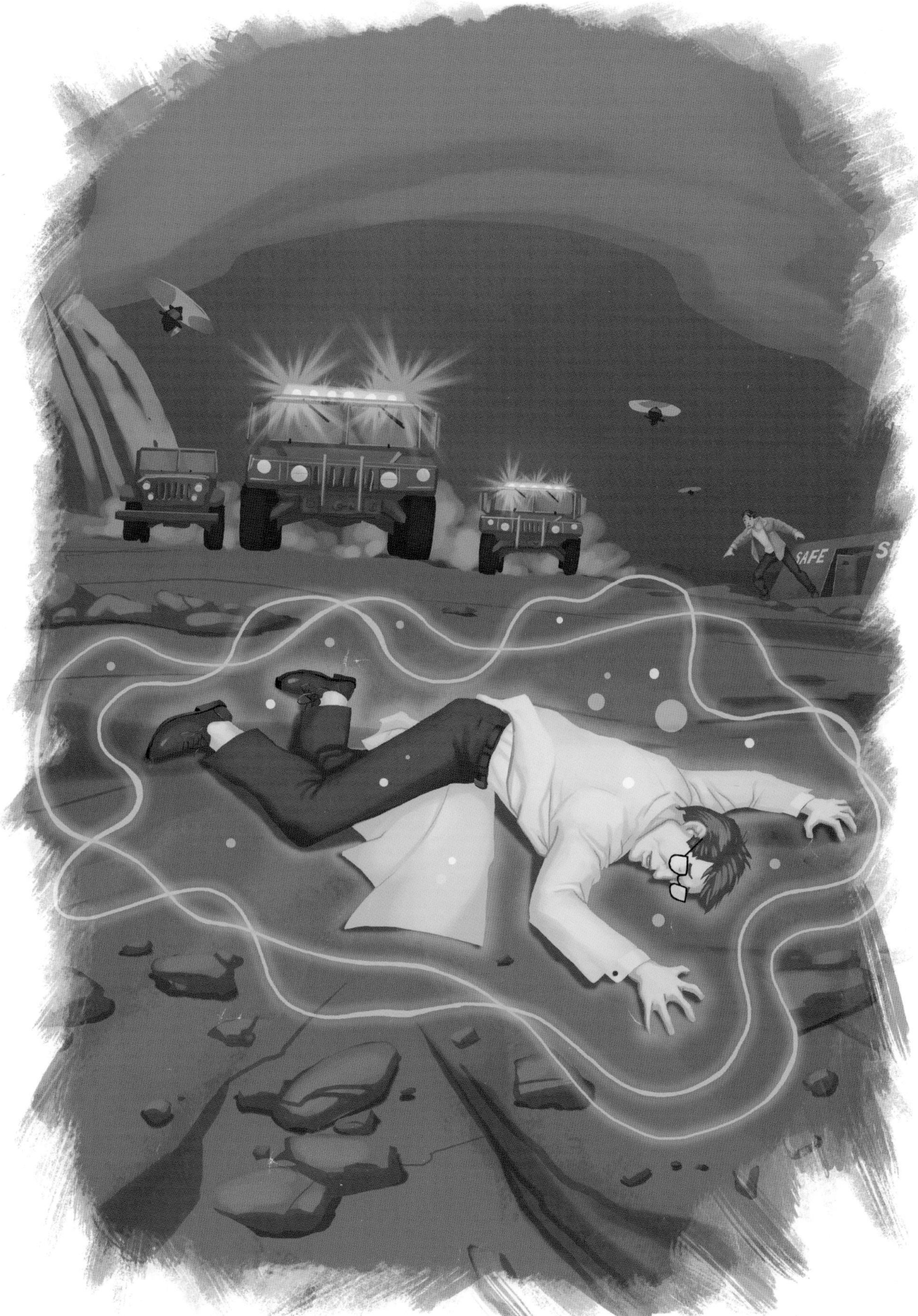
SAFE

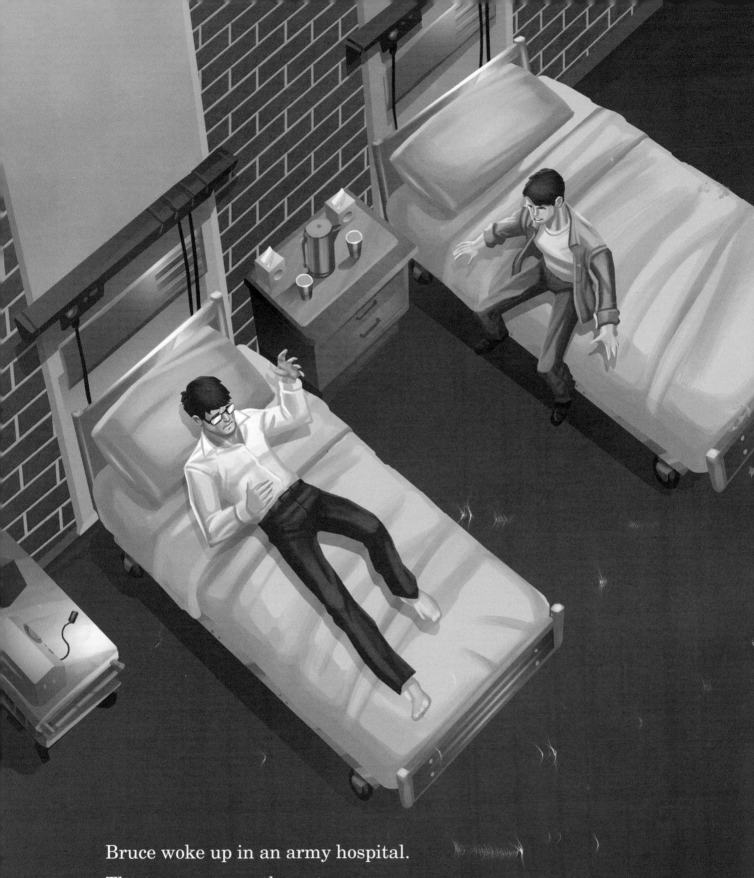

Bruce woke up in an army hospital.

The teenager was there, too.

Bruce learned the boy's name was **RICK JONES.**

Rick thanked Bruce for saving his life.

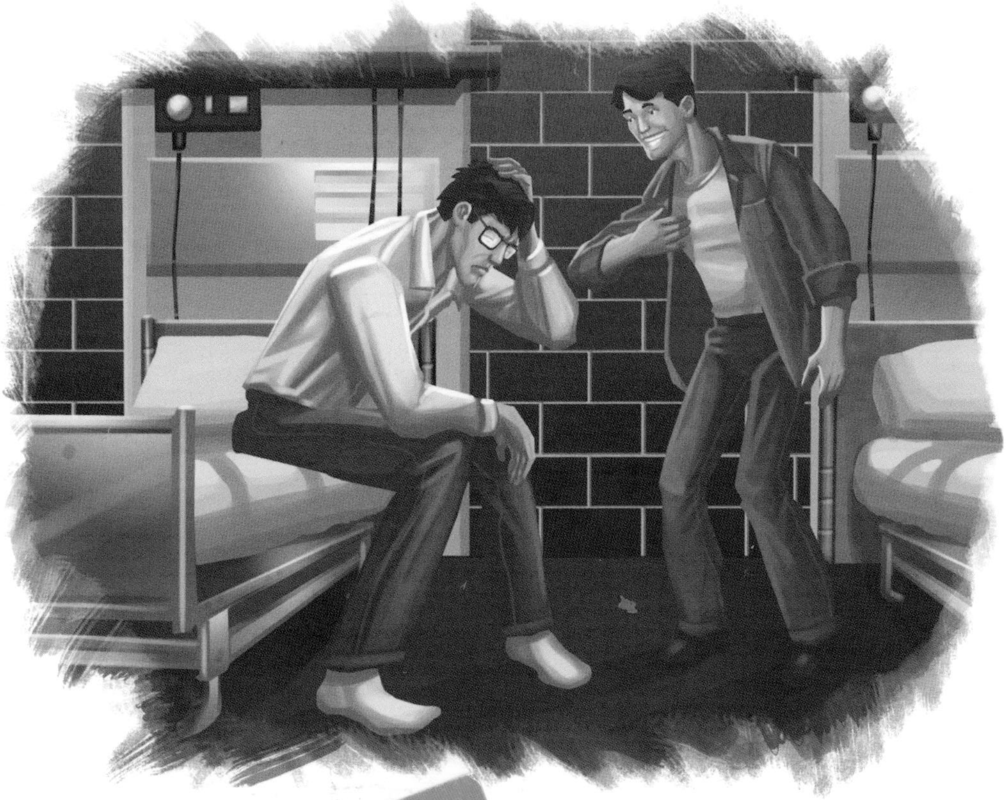

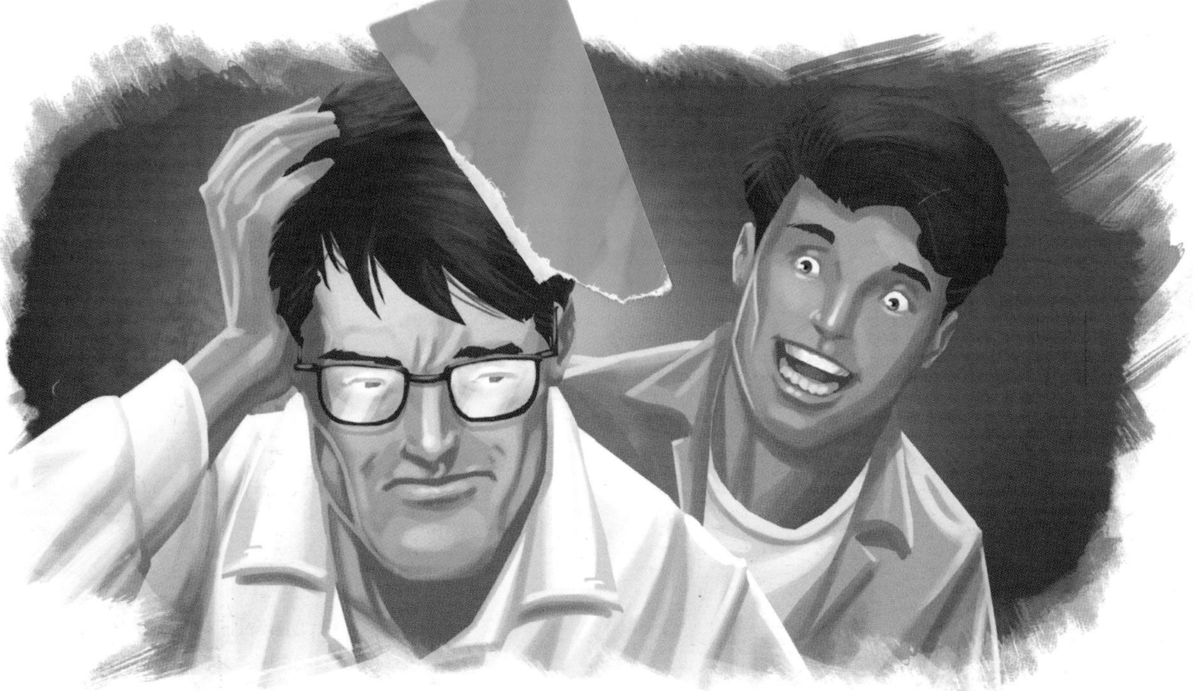

Bruce was happy that Rick was safe.

He was also happy to be alive.

But then he looked around.

He was locked up.

He remembered the blast.

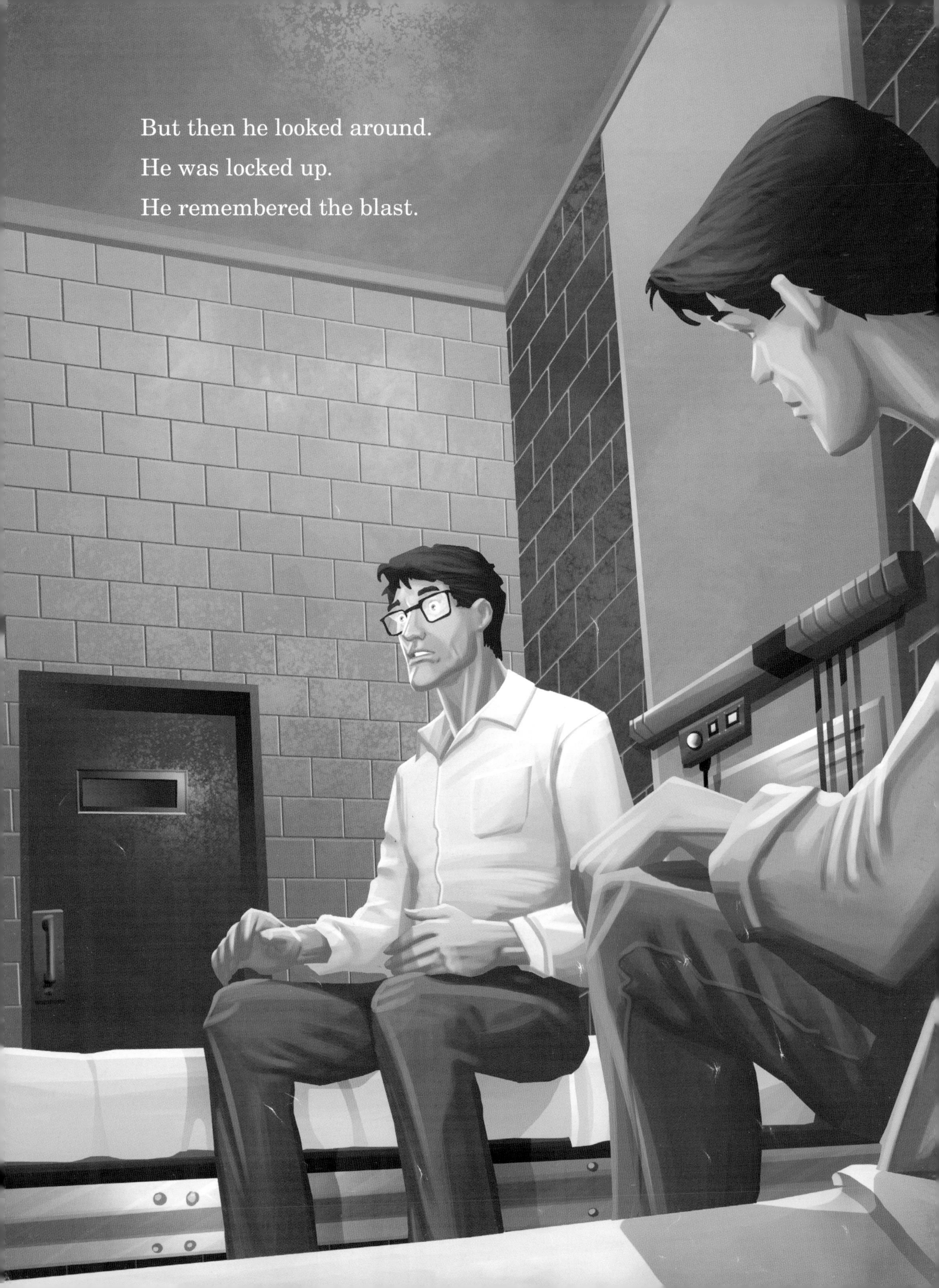

He felt so scared, so confused,
and so helpless.

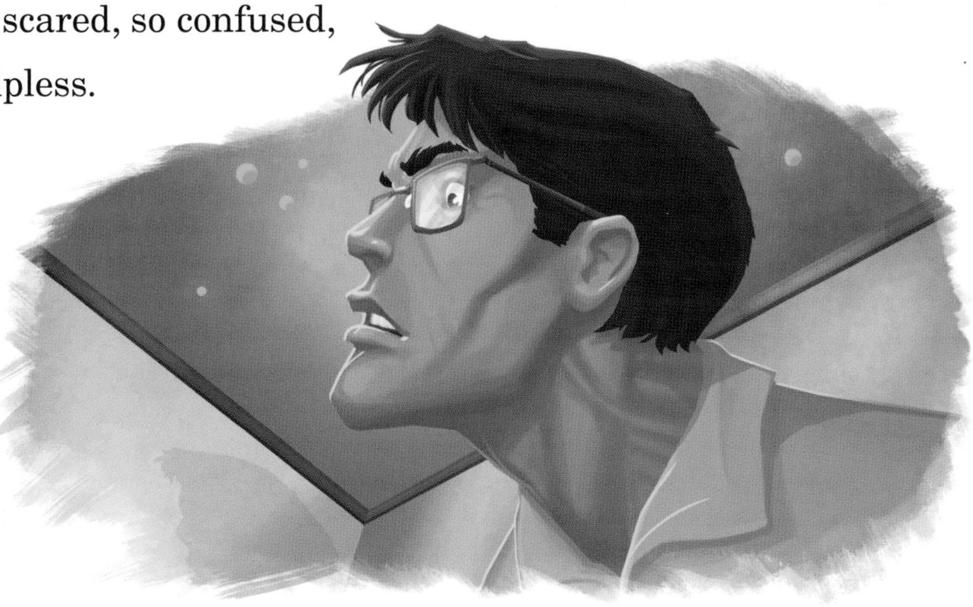

Just the way he had when
he was young.

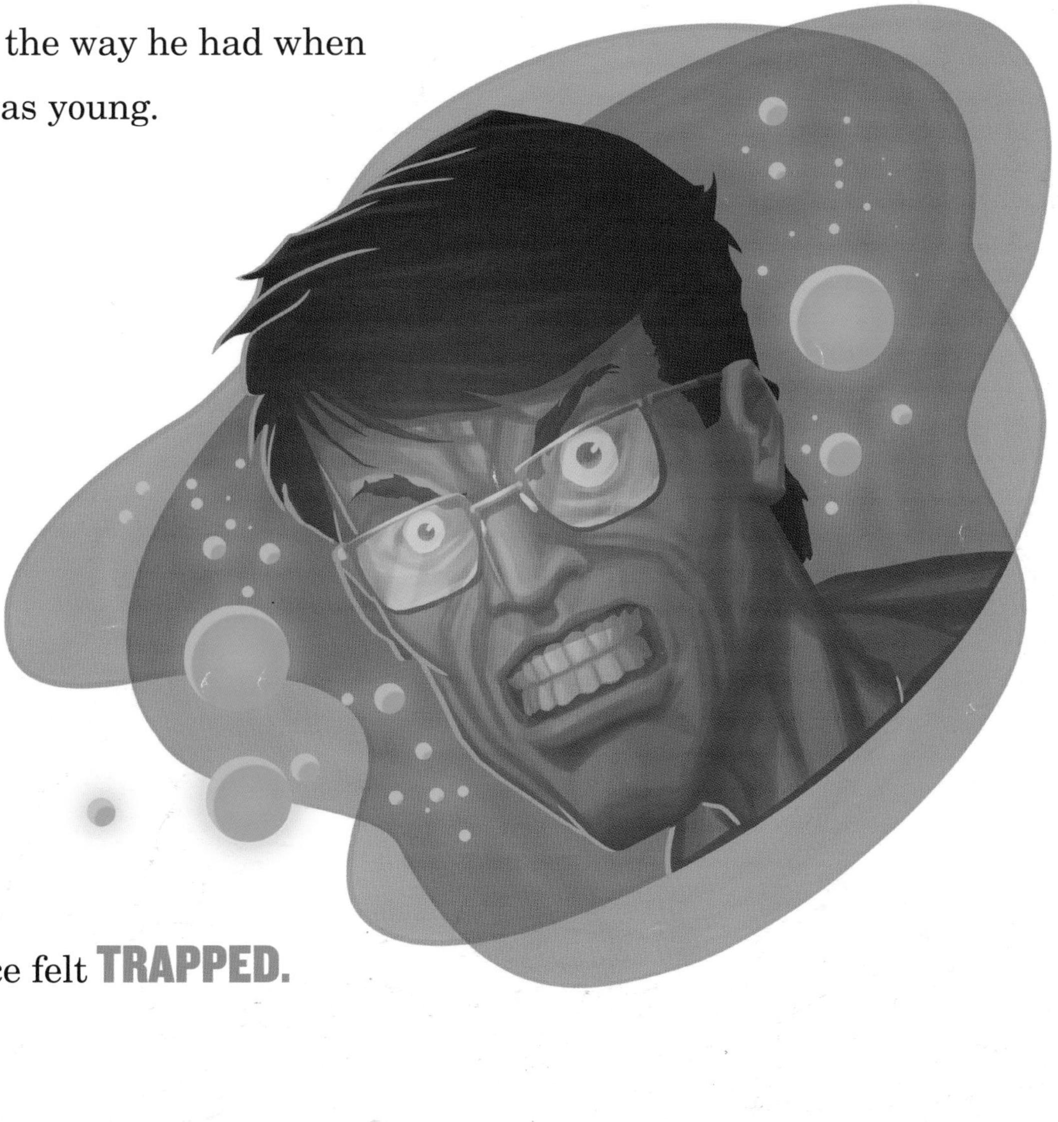

Bruce felt **TRAPPED.**

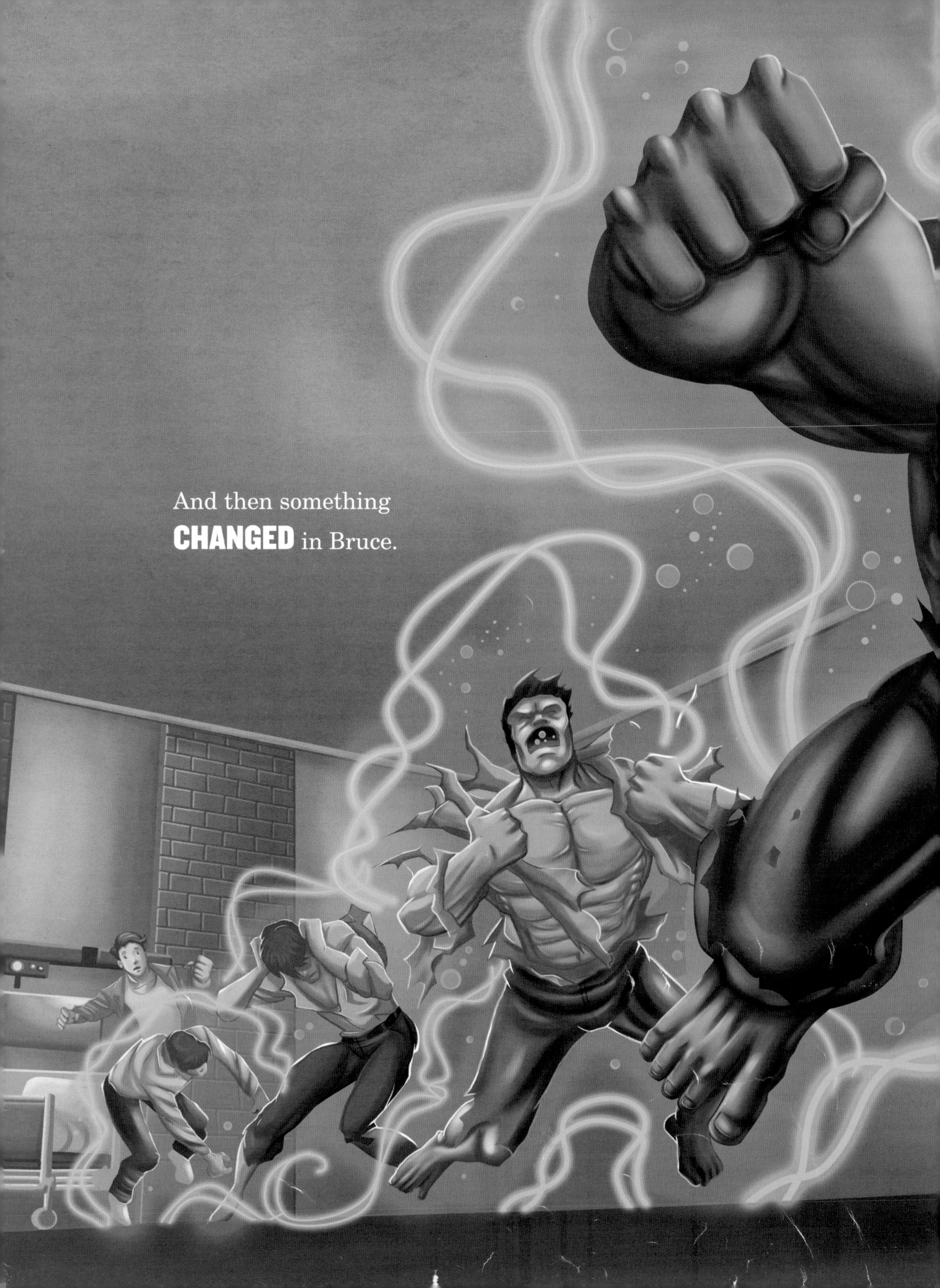

And then something **CHANGED** in Bruce.

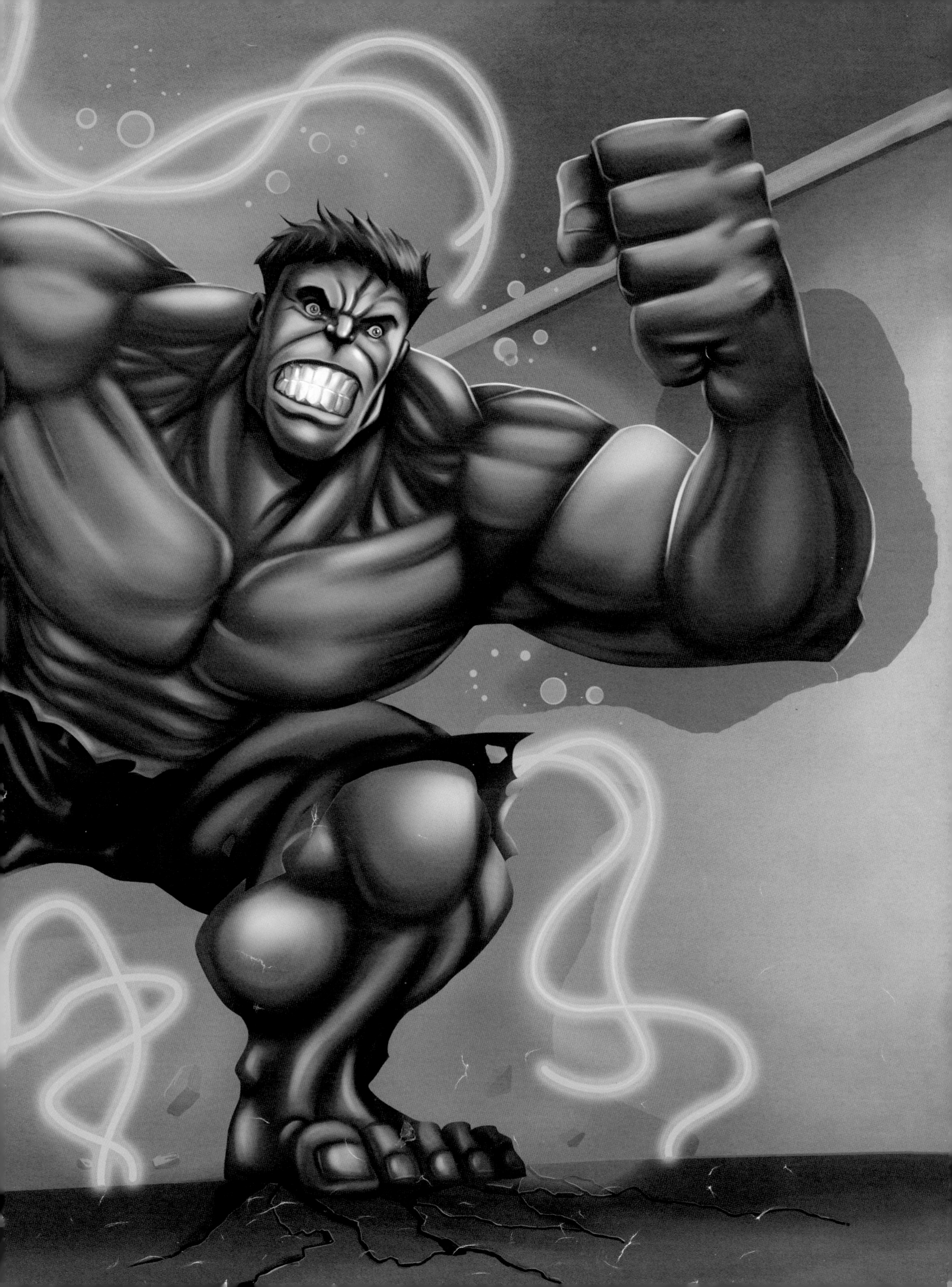

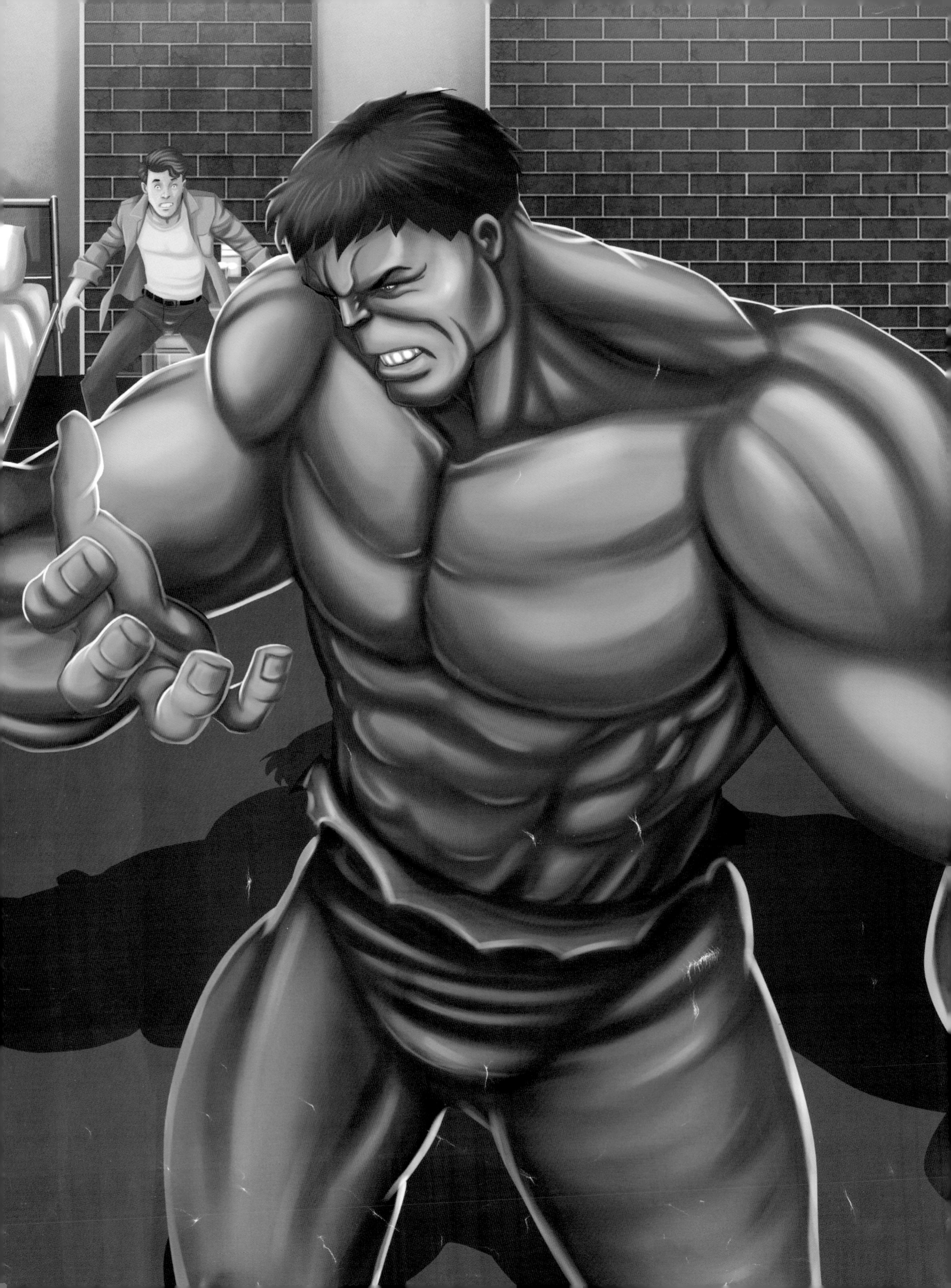

The soldiers didn't know that the gamma rays had transformed Bruce!

They didn't recognize Bruce. They called him a . . .

. . . HULK!

The army tried to stop the Hulk.
But the Hulk just wanted to leave.

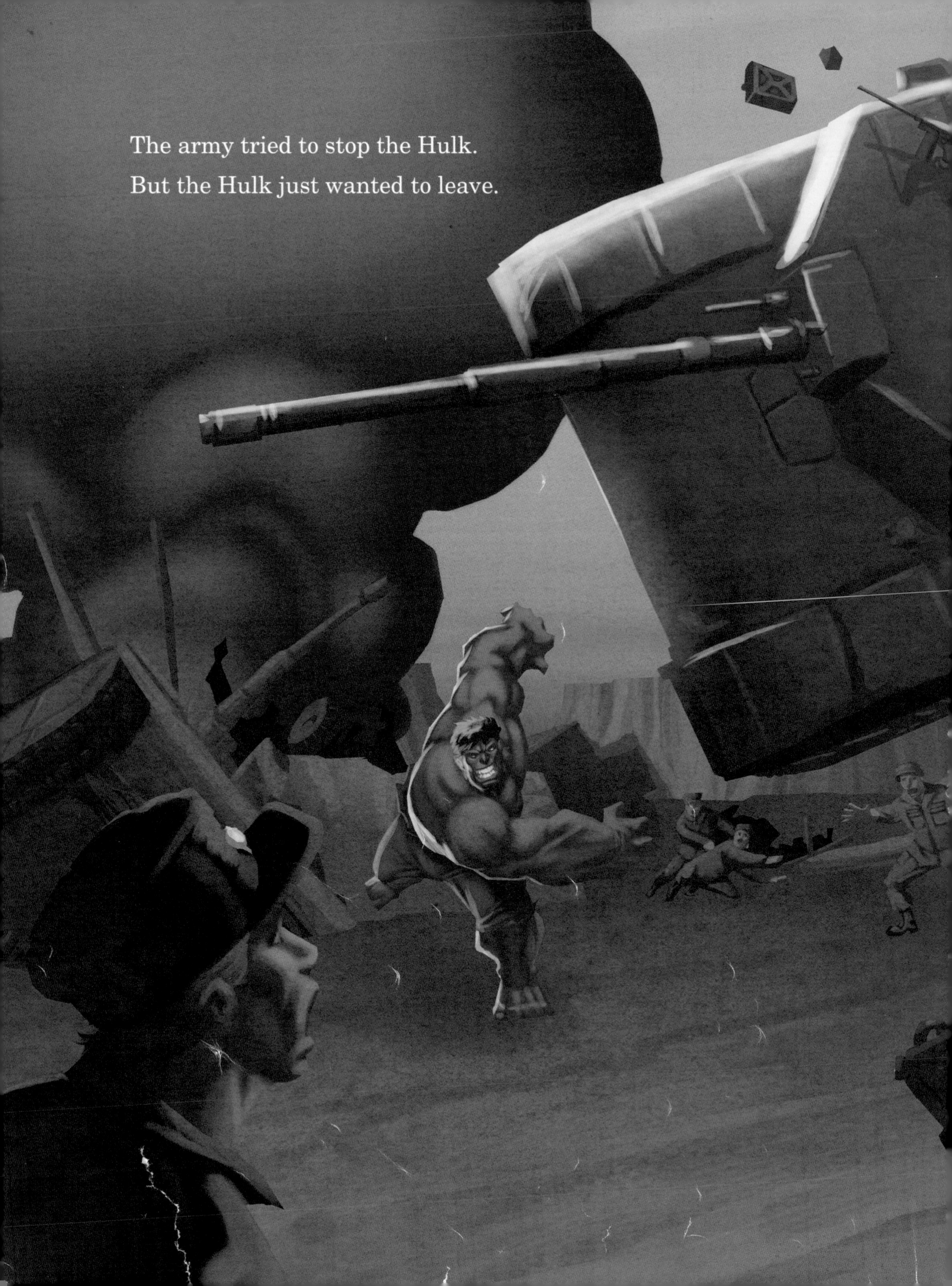

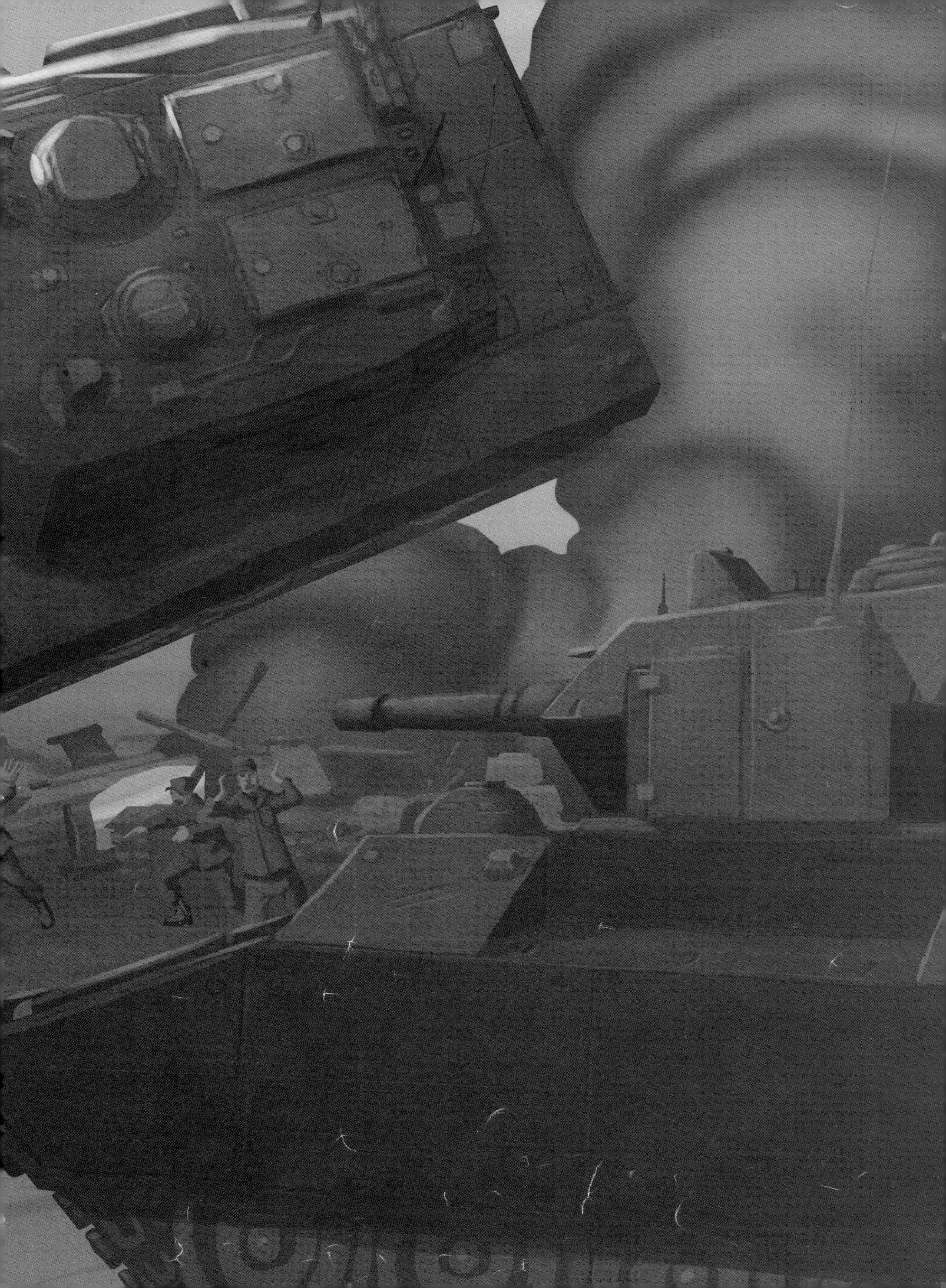

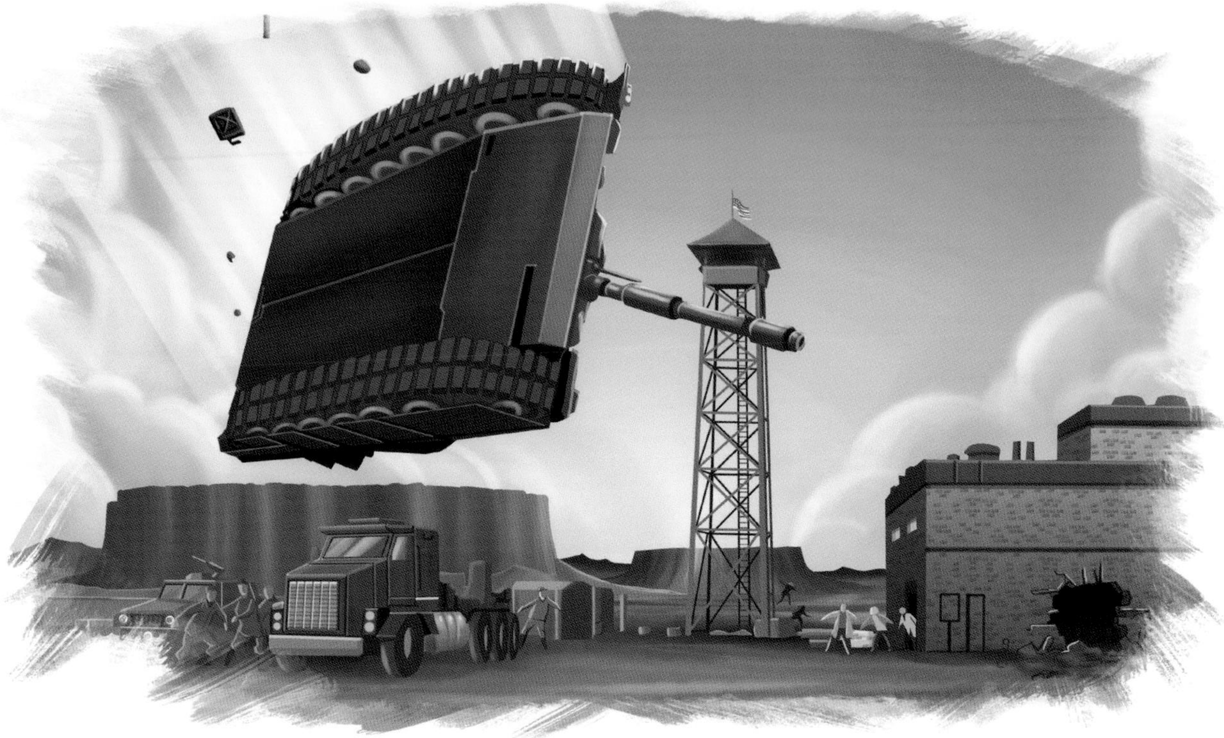

He didn't want to hurt anyone.
He only wanted to be left alone.

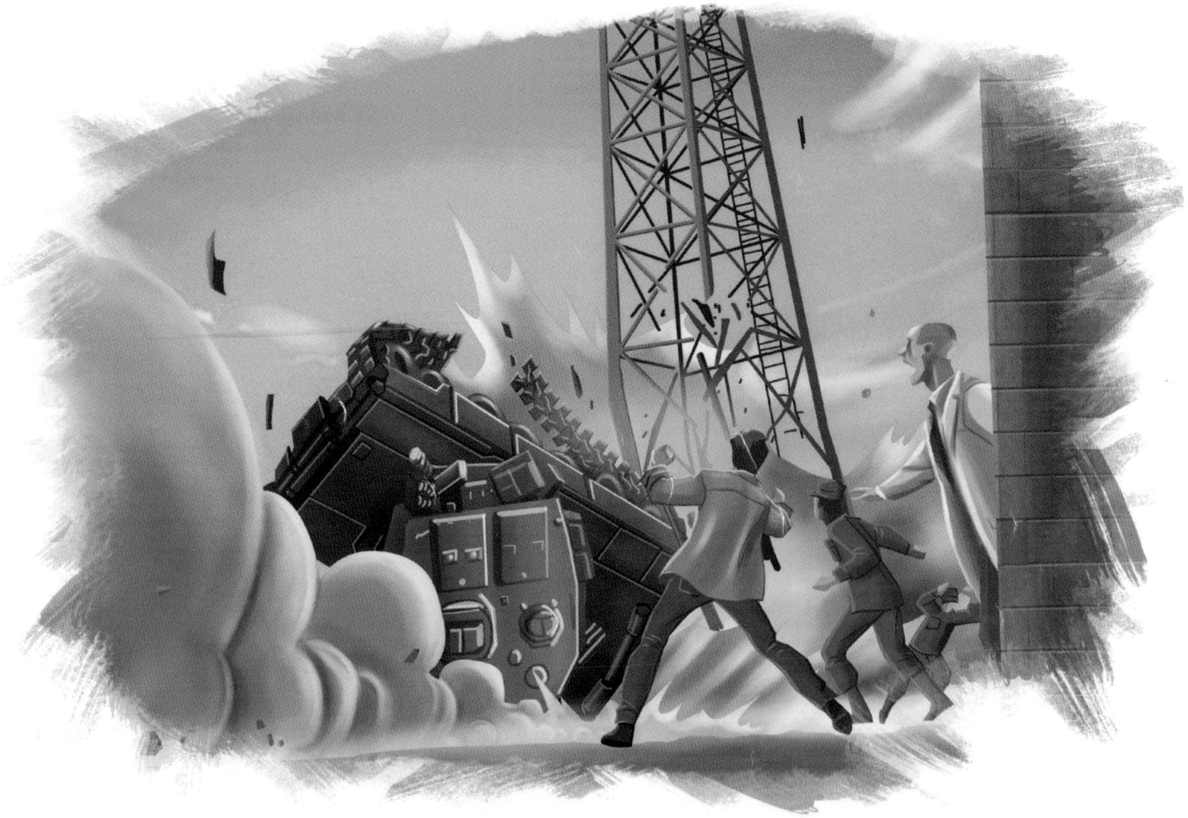

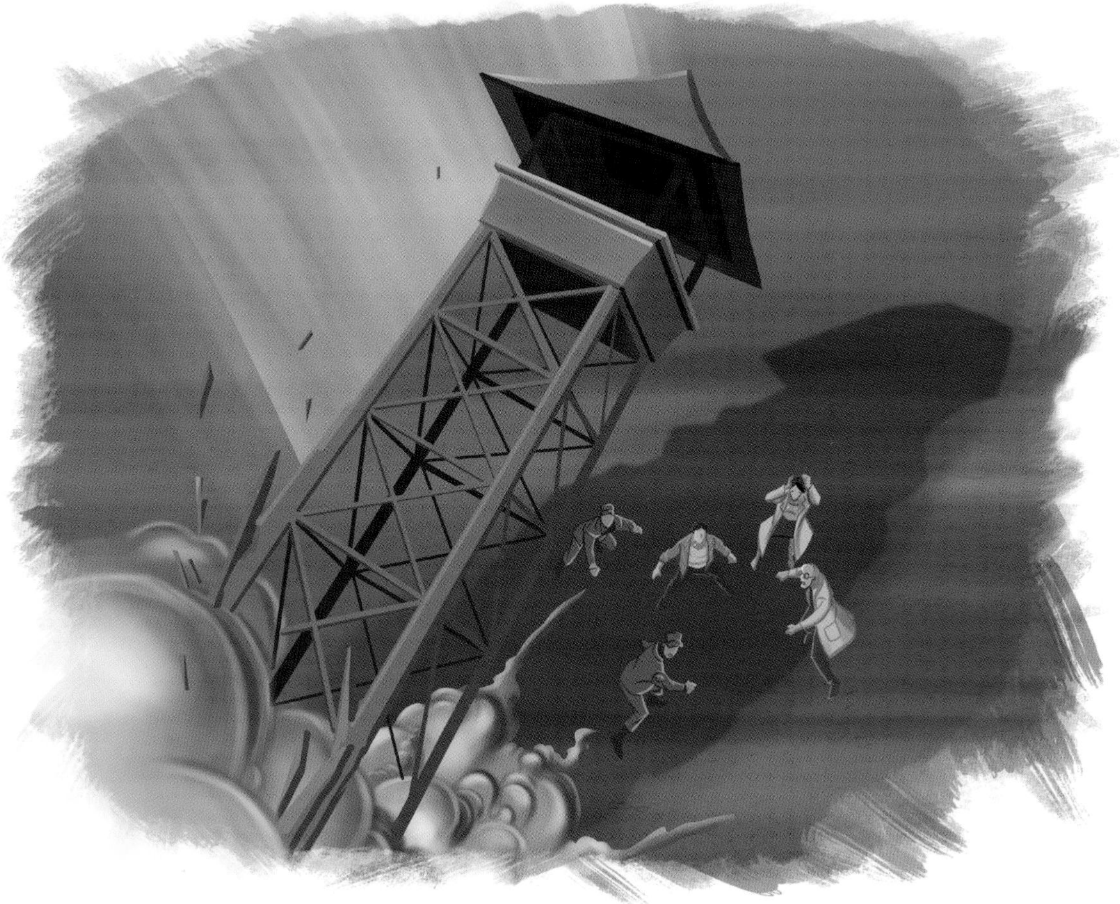

So when he noticed that his actions
put the soldiers in harm's way . . .

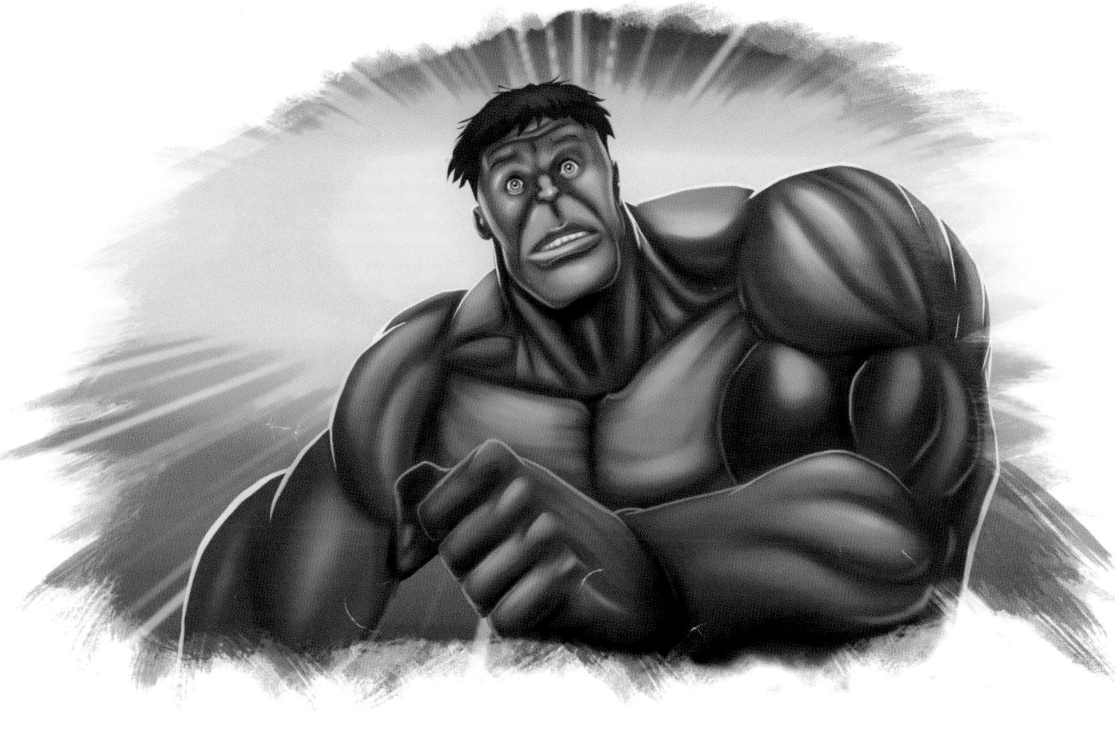

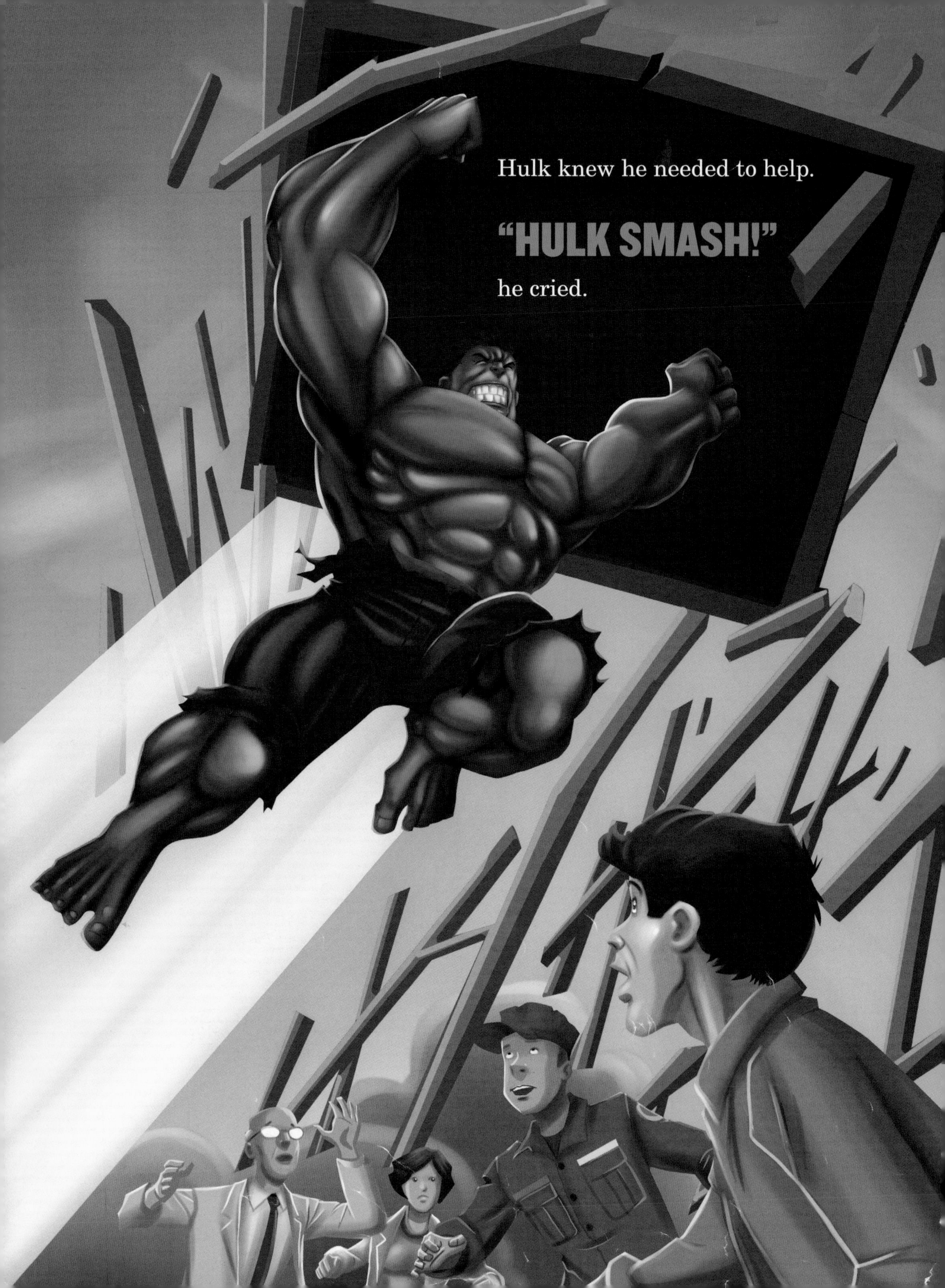

Hulk knew he needed to help.

"HULK SMASH!"

he cried.

The Hulk had saved the soldiers . . .

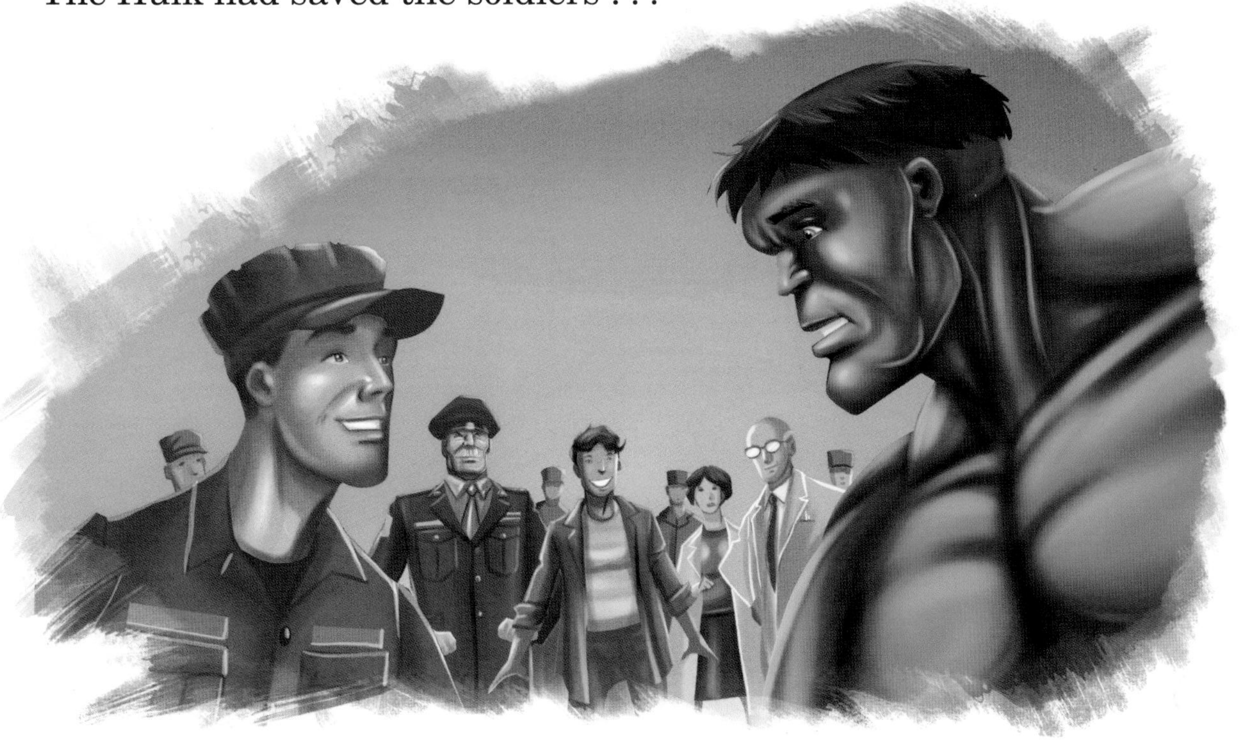

. . . and leaped away before he did any more damage.

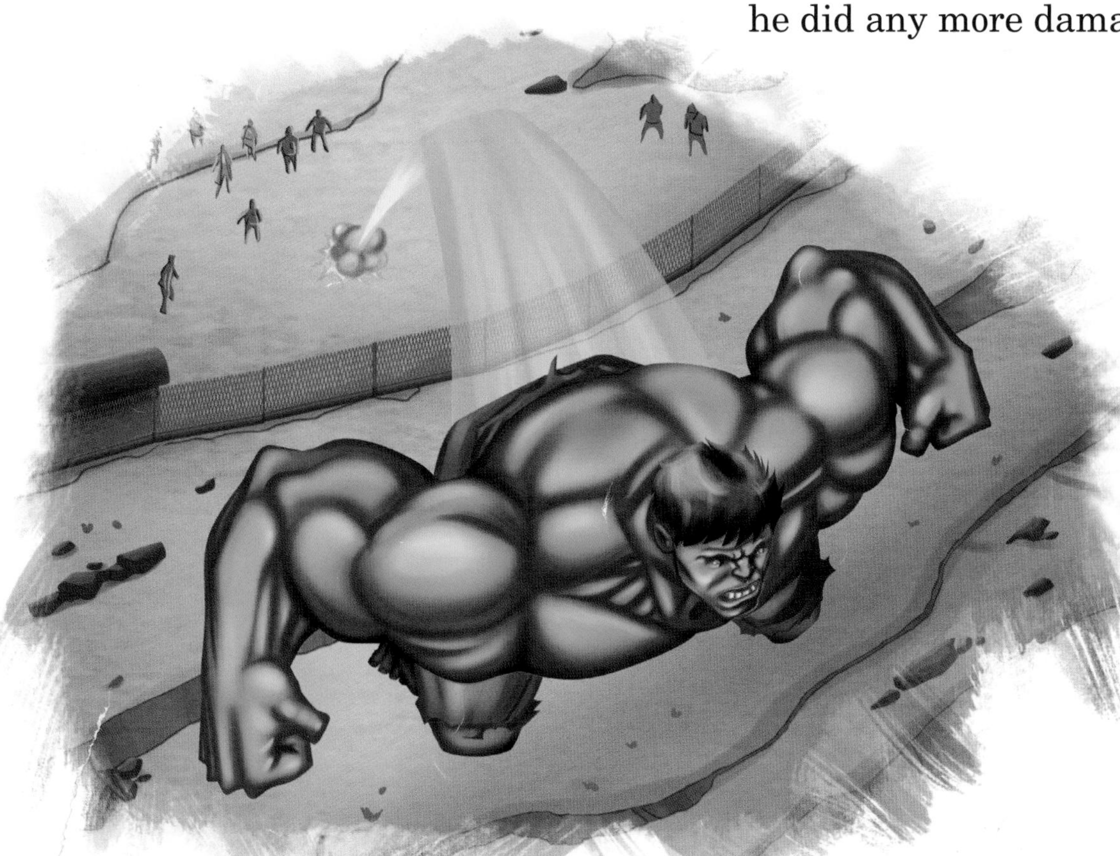

And not long after . . .

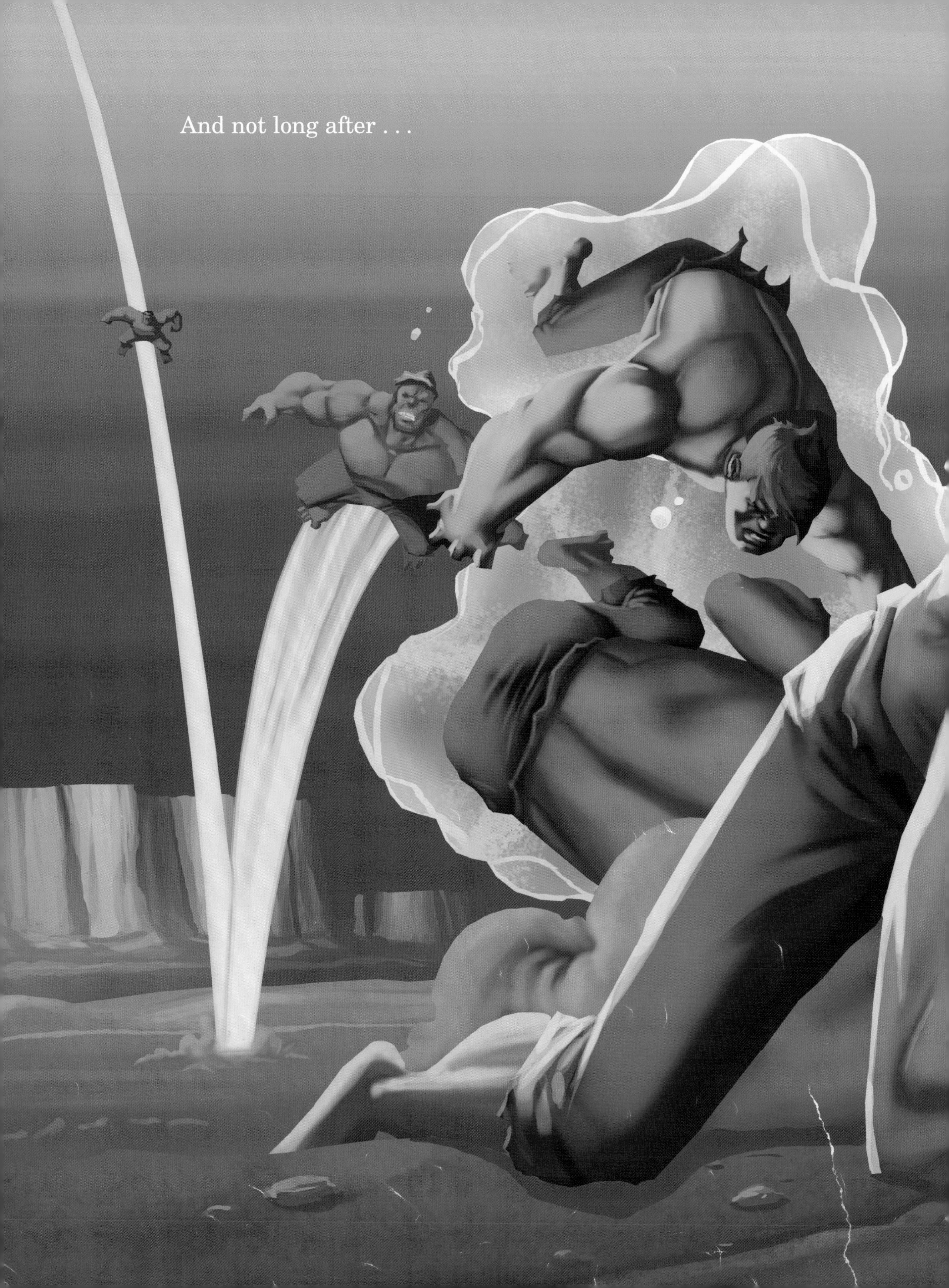

. . . he transformed back into **BRUCE BANNER.**

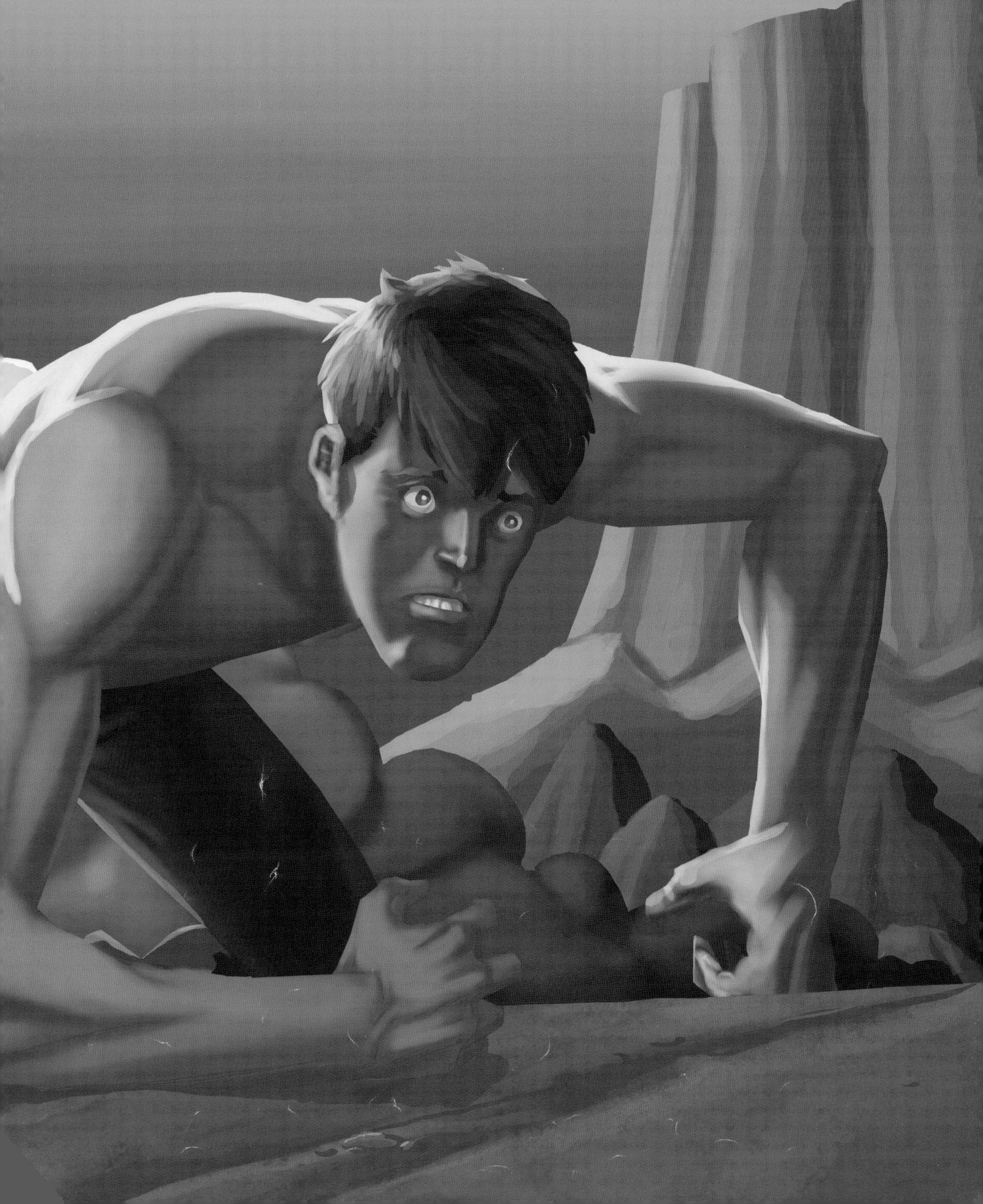

Bruce didn't know if he would ever change
into the Hulk again.
He thought it best to hide out and lay low.

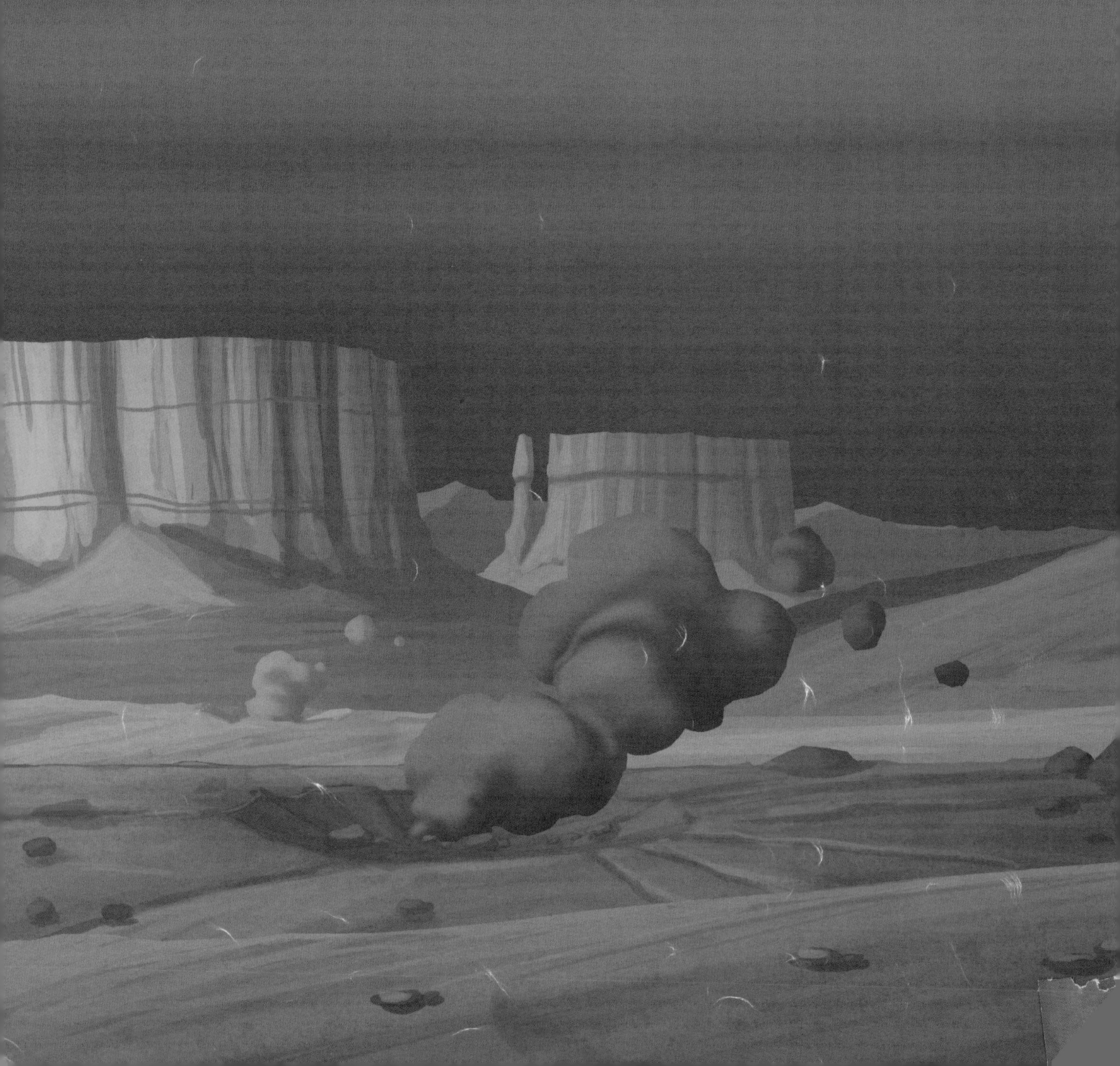

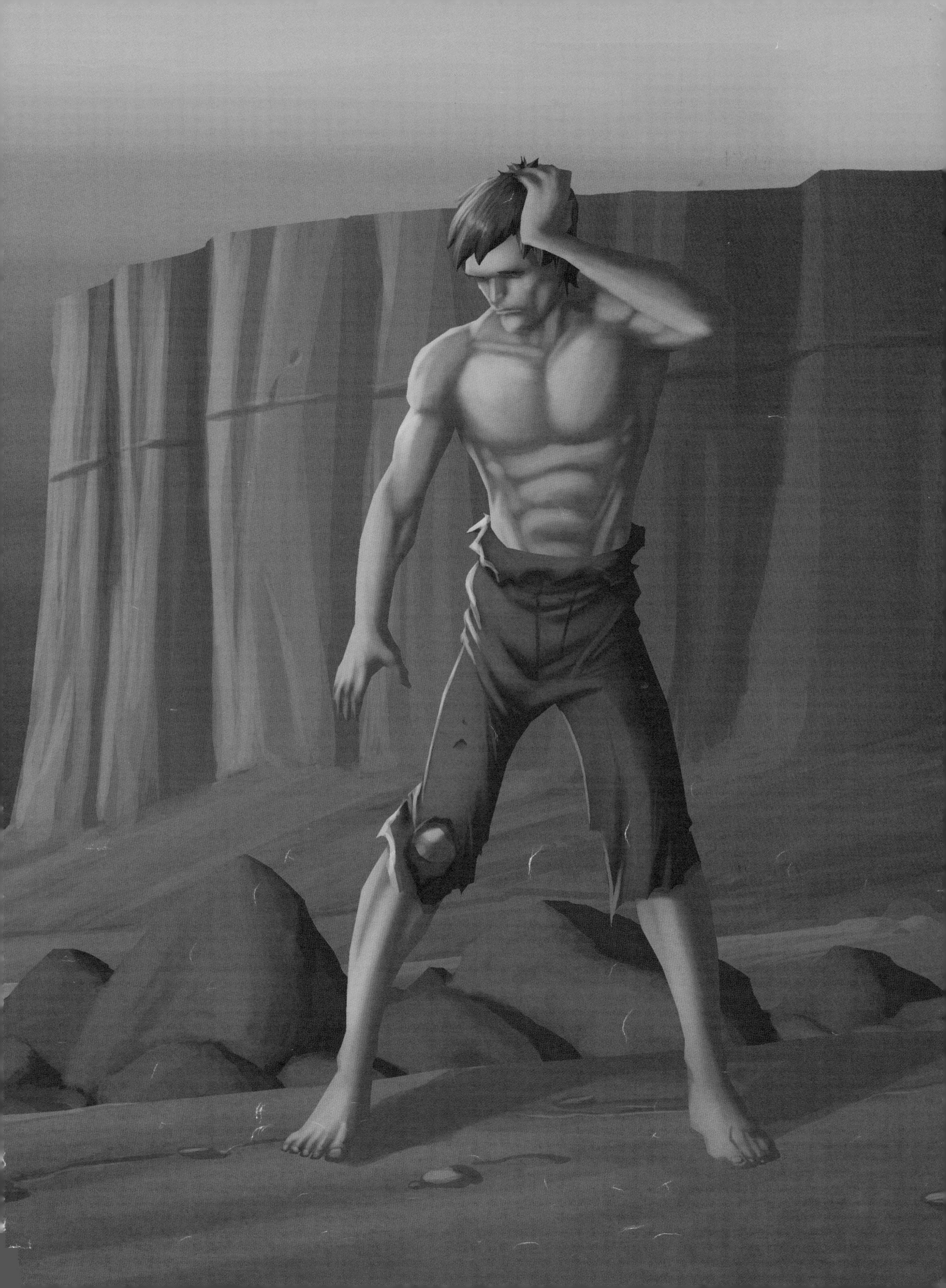

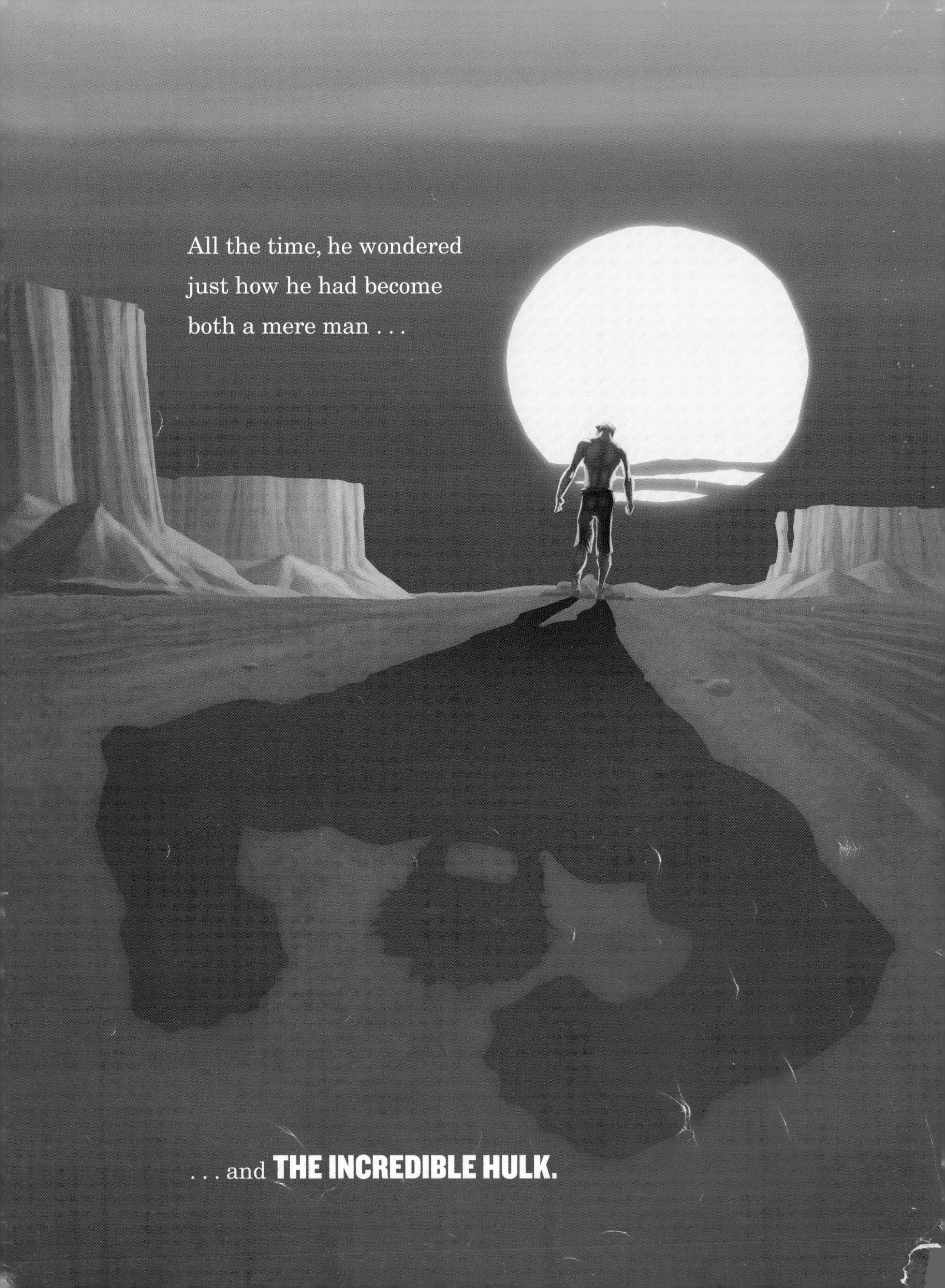

All the time, he wondered
just how he had become
both a mere man . . .

. . . and **THE INCREDIBLE HULK.**